What was he doing here?

Pierce stopped his car, realizing that he'd ended up outside the office complex that housed KXPG Radio. Every night he felt as if Georgia was speaking directly to him, when in fact she was reaching out to thousands. He was nuts to believe any sort of connection existed between them.

Georgia shared a final bit of poetry before signing off. Pierce had no interest in the radio after that, preferring silence to the insipid programming that followed *Seattle after Midnight.*

He eyed the parking lot and wondered which of the handful of vehicles sitting there at five in the morning belonged to Georgia. *Oh, for Pete's sake. Just go home, would you?*

He didn't. And fifteen minutes later his tenacity was rewarded as a woman who could only be Georgia dashed out of the building. The security guard had held the outer door open for her and continued to watch after her as she raced for her car. Pierce opened his window in time to hear her call out, "Thanks, Monty. I'm fine."

The security guard waved, then returned to his post. No sooner had the door swung shut behind him than Georgia let out a scream.

Dear Reader,

Have you ever been awake at night when everyone—almost the entire world, it seems—is asleep? The world looks different in the dark, doesn't it? It feels different, too. Somehow our fears, anxieties and insecurities seem to thrive in the shadows.

The late-night radio host understands the world of the dark. She knows about insomniacs, shift workers and night owls. With carefully selected music and her own specially chosen words, she reaches through the night and makes connections with these people.

Georgia Lamont is the host of *Seattle after Midnight*. She has a talent for connecting with her listeners. But what happens when she makes a connection with the wrong person? This is the question I asked myself when I began to write this story. But even as I began to explore the sinister side of the night, another question formed in my mind.

What happens when she makes a connection with the right person—someone who needs her as much as she needs him?

I hope you enjoy this story. If you would like to write or send e-mail, I would be delighted to hear from you through my Web site at www.cjcarmichael.com. Or send mail to #1754-246 Stewart Green, S.W., Calgary, Alberta, T3H 3C8, Canada.

Sincerely,

C.J. *Carmichael*

Seattle after Midnight
C.J. Carmichael

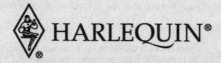

HARLEQUIN®

TORONTO • NEW YORK • LONDON
AMSTERDAM • PARIS • SYDNEY • HAMBURG
STOCKHOLM • ATHENS • TOKYO • MILAN • MADRID
PRAGUE • WARSAW • BUDAPEST • AUCKLAND

ISBN 0-373-71240-5

SEATTLE AFTER MIDNIGHT

Copyright © 2004 by Carla Daum.

This edition published by arrangement with Harlequin Books S.A.

www.eHarlequin.com

Printed in U.S.A.

The author would like to thank her friend,
audiophile Mike Fitzpatrick, for being her music consultant
for this project and for introducing her
to the bliss of Kenny Rankin.

Christina Rowsell (host of *Christina After Dark*),
thank you for your generosity in inviting me to your studio,
answering my questions and introducing me to the
fascinating, multitasking, crazy world of radio.

For my brother Phil

Books by C.J. Carmichael

HARLEQUIN SUPERROMANCE

Don't miss any of our special offers. Write to us at the
following address for information on our newest releases.

Harlequin Reader Service
U.S.: 3010 Walden Ave., P.O. Box 1325, Buffalo, NY 14269
Canadian: P.O. Box 609, Fort Erie, Ont. L2A 5X3

CHAPTER ONE

"IT'S AFTER MIDNIGHT, Seattle. You know what that means, don't you?"

The voice, seductive and yet somehow comforting, propelled Pierce Harding to crank up the volume of his radio, so he could hear above the steady drumming of rain on the roof of his car.

"You're listening to Georgia and this is *Seattle after Midnight* on KXPG radio…."

Across the street the Charleston Hotel sparkled with seasonal fairy lights. A wreath decked out with bows and fake fruit made the oak entrance look Christmas-card perfect.

Pierce popped a square of chewing gum out of a pack and into his mouth. It was the beginning of December and Christmas was being rammed down his throat wherever he turned. He could only hope Georgia wouldn't play any bloody carols on her show tonight.

Parked with the owner's permission at the service end of a gas station, Pierce had a clear view up and down the street. The sidewalks were deserted. Occasionally a car would drive by. Only three had stopped for gas in the past half hour.

Thanks to the cold, he had to keep the windows closed and run the heater at fifteen-minute intervals to clear the condensation. But even with the pumped-in warmth, he felt chilled. Tired. Alone.

"This is your time," the radio host promised. She sounded a bit like Demi Moore, Pierce thought. Only sexier, if that was possible.

"Yours and mine," she continued, her voice dipping even deeper. "I have some sweet surprises in store for you, so stay with Georgia and we'll get through this night together, I promise."

Across the street the door to the hotel opened. Pierce grabbed his video recorder and hit the power button. But the two people holding hands as they dashed for a waiting taxi were strangers. He set down the camera and prepared himself mentally for a long wait.

His agency had been hired to keep twenty-four-hour surveillance on the wife of a man who was out of town on business for three days. Jodi and Steven Calder were in their midforties, childless and wealthy. Steven—Pierce's client—suspected Jodi of having an affair. A suspicion that seemed likely to be true.

Just four hours ago Jodi had taken a taxi from the Calder's estate home in Madison Park. She'd had a big black suitcase with her and when the cab had pulled up in front of the Charleston, Pierce had been sure she was up to no good.

But as far as he could tell, she was in her room alone and had been for hours. He'd been keeping an eye out for single males entering the hotel, but had seen none. The Charleston seemed to appeal more to older couples and families than the business crowd.

Or the illicit-lovers crowd.

What was Jodi Calder doing in that hotel room? Had her lover been delayed somehow? Had he canceled? But if that were the case, why hadn't Jodi Calder returned to her comfortable home?

The situation was puzzling, but soon would become someone else's problem. He'd broken the watch into three eight-hour stretches. Jake Jeffrey, his youngest and newest employee, would be covering mornings, starting at 5:00 a.m. Will Livingstone, the senior man in Pierce's team, would handle the afternoon shift.

If Jodi Calder's lover ever did turn up, they'd catch him, all right.

"Tonight we're going to play something special." Georgia's voice sounded as close and intimate as if she were sitting in his car with him. "When Kenny Rankin sings in the key of D minor, the result is something no feeling person could ever forget. Imagine you're at a table in a Parisian bistro, sipping wine and thinking of that one person you've never been able to forget."

The music started then, plaintive notes, a pleasing melody, then a man's voice, clear and pure.

Pierce's chest welled with an unrecognizable sensation, a sweet aching. More and more he felt this way when he listened to Georgia's show and he couldn't help but wonder if this was the emotion Cass had tried to describe to him in the years they'd been married.

She'd been so good to him, tried so patiently to help him, and he'd given precious little in exchange.

Cass, I thought I loved you.

But the way he felt right now, he knew something had been missing. And Cass had known, too.

"Beautiful, isn't it?" Georgia said as the song ended. "Tonight we're going to be listening to a lot of music played in those sad, haunting minor keys. Because we all know that love isn't always sunshine and roses. If you can relate to that, I want to hear from you. Give me a call, toll-free, at…"

As she recited the phone number, Pierce imagined what it would be like to call Georgia, to actually speak to her.

He shook his head, amazed that the idea had even crossed his mind. He muttered the toll-free number that Georgia repeated frequently throughout her program. So frequently he had it memorized. His fingers itched for the cell phone in his jacket pocket.

God, he was worse than an obsessed teenager.

Keep your mind on the job, he reminded himself.

He'd gone thirty years without falling in love. He certainly wasn't about to start now, with a woman he'd never even met.

FIFTEEN-YEAR-OLD Brady Walsh couldn't sleep, which was nothing unusual. He was often awake for hours after his mother said good-night to him, usually around ten o'clock. It was their unspoken agreement that as long as he stayed in his room, she wouldn't interfere with whatever he chose to do— homework, surfing the Internet, or playing video games.

On weeknights after twelve he listened to the radio. He'd found a new program he really liked. The music was kind of hokey, but the disk jockey was really cool. Listening to Georgia he forgot about the fact that he had no friends, no girlfriend, no life.

And no wonder.

Brady stood in front of his bedroom window. With his bedside lamp on, and the big oak outside screening the streetlamps, the glass was perfectly reflective, showing in excruciating detail all the reasons he would forever be a nerd.

Too tall, too skinny, too many zits. Braces on his teeth. Then there was his nose. Brady put a hand up to his most hated feature. It was the same as his father's and though he knew his dad had been considered a good-looking man in his day, on Brady the nose looked gargantuan.

He wasn't surprised Courtney wouldn't talk to him anymore.

He went to his desk, where he kept his old junior high yearbook open to page twenty-five and a photograph of the drama club. In the center of the group of students—most of them girls—was Courtney herself, her blond hair gleaming, her perfect teeth, which had never needed braces, showcased in her heart-stopping smile.

Courtney. She was so far out of his league—in looks, personality and popularity—that he never would have dared to dream about her if they hadn't been assigned to the same research project at the start of the school year.

He'd been surprised at how smart she was, how easy to get along with, how funny. She contributed ideas, but was willing to listen to his suggestions, too. They'd met after school for three precious afternoons, and one Friday evening at her house, her mother had ordered pizza and they'd worked until after nine.

She laughed easily and often, but not foolishly like so many of the girls at school.

They'd aced the project. Got the highest mark in the class.

Restless, Brady paced his room, not sure what to do with his energy. It was well past midnight, but he knew he'd never sleep. His room was beginning to feel like a cell.

Gently, he eased the door open. His mother had stopped crying about half an hour ago. Her door was shut and no light showed in the gap between door and carpet.

He slipped downstairs and raided the fridge of that night's leftovers. As he munched on a piece of roast shoved into a crusty dinner roll, he noticed his mother's purse on the counter next to the phone. Beside the purse was the key holder for her new Audi.

The car had been a birthday present from his father in June. That was six months ago and she'd driven the car only a handful of times, preferring to get around in his dad's old Buick.

Brady could hardly wait until he had his driver's license. His mother had already told him she'd let him use the Audi whenever he wanted. What freedom that would be! He imagined himself at the wheel, the window rolled down, a fresh breeze in his hair.

The first place he'd go would be Courtney's house. He remembered where she lived, had even figured out which window belonged to her room.

An urgent longing to see her, right this second, hit him. If he drove by her house, maybe the light in her room would be on. Maybe he'd catch her silhouette as she walked past the window to her bed…

He stared at the key holder that he had no legal right to touch. He had only a learner's permit. The car wasn't his.

Then he scooped the black plastic case up and pressed the silver button on the side. The key sprang out like a secret weapon. Cool. He felt like he could tap into the power of the V-8 engine just from this slender piece of metal.

Why not? An inner voice challenged. *How would Mom ever find out? Just don't go too far, don't use too much gas and you won't have any problems.*

Brady tossed the key into the air once, then grinned. He was going to do this.

Five minutes later, he was in his mother's car. He glanced over the dashboard, familiarizing himself with the various controls. The car came equipped with a cell phone. That could come in handy, too.

Nervous, but determined, Brady reversed out of the garage. On the radio the woman with the throaty voice welcomed him back to *Seattle after Midnight*. He thought about what she'd said earlier. *Imagine you're at a table in a Parisian bistro, sipping wine and thinking of that one person....*

Clear as daylight, he saw that person. For a moment he had to close his eyes, choke back tears.

Courtney, he reminded himself. *I have to check out her house.* Tentatively he opened his eyes. Tried clearing his throat, then singing along to the song on the radio.

He was fine. Everything was under control. He turned on the windshield wipers, then hit the button on the visor to close the garage. He was more determined than ever to get away from this place. Carefully, he eased onto the road, then switched gears and nosed the car down the lane.

STANDING AT the window in her darkened living room, Sylvie Moreau watched until the taillights of her lover's car had disappeared around a corner. Feeling a confused mixture of relief and disappointment, she dropped the curtain into place and retreated to her kitchen.

The countertops were spotless. Reid had cleaned up from the feast he'd brought with him—take-out sushi and chocolate-covered strawberries. He'd even rinsed the empty bottle of champagne and disposed of it in her recycle bin on the back step.

Reid was considerate, both out of bed and in, and Sylvie still considered it a small miracle that she'd ever met him. At the very least it had been a fluke. A couple of months ago at her favorite bookstore, she'd noticed him in line ahead of her for a coffee. Later she'd found that he'd never been to the store before in his life, and had only stopped in on impulse.

They'd started chatting and had eventually taken their coffees to a small table where the conversation had continued to flow as if they'd known each other forever.

Of course, she'd noticed he wore a wedding ring, but that first meeting had been so innocent. When he'd asked her to lunch, she'd assumed his intentions were merely friendly. And probably that was all he had been interested in, at first, for them to just be friends.

But for over a month now, they'd been more than friends and she'd never been happier.

Or unhappier.

Strange how opposite emotions could coexist in one body. In truth, the ups and downs were somewhat addictive. They kept her from thinking about her past—her mother's death, then her own aborted engagement, and the miserable years after.

Sylvie turned off the main floor lights and headed upstairs to her bedroom. Six months ago, on her thirtieth birthday, she'd come into her inheritance from an income-trust on her father's side of the family. Her first step had been to buy this house, a cute little Victorian on Queen Anne Hill. Then, she'd quit her job, a move that with hindsight had been a mistake. Without the daily interaction with her co-workers at the bank, she'd felt more lonely than ever.

Until Reid.

Sylvie switched the house sound system from CD to radio, then twisted on the taps to her Jacuzzi tub, adding a handful of lavender-scented salts. She dropped her satin robe in a cloth-lined hamper, then disposed of the matching teddy in a similar manner.

Sylvie slipped into the warm bath water. As soon

as she turned off the taps she was able to hear again the radio program playing softly.

She always listened to KXPG, but her favorite program, by far, was this late-night show hosted by a radio personality named Georgia. Georgia was new to Seattle, had only been on the air a few months, but already Sylvie was addicted to the eclectic selection of music and the thoughtful musings and opinions of the host.

"Imagine you're at a table in a Parisian bistro," Georgia invited her, "sipping wine and thinking of that one person you've never been able to forget…."

Sylvie sighed and closed her eyes. The fragrant candles she'd lit for Reid were still burning and the sweet scent added to the quiet mood of the night. Georgia's question lingered in her mind. Who was the one person she would never forget?

Her ex-fiancé, Wayne? No way. He hadn't been able to understand the deep depression she'd slid into after her mother's funeral. Though she'd been mortified when he'd broken their engagement, now she was glad she hadn't married him.

So was Reid the love of her life, then? But what about his wife? She blanked her mind, as she always did when she hit this particular wall. As Reid said, all that mattered was that they loved each other. Goodness knew, she loved him. And she truly believed that he loved her, too.

If only she could forget about his wife. And the two kids who called him Daddy.

AT FOUR-THIRTY in the morning Jake Jeffrey drove up to the gas station for his shift. Pierce opened the car door and met Jake in the parking lot. Jake was young and eager and listened raptly as Pierce gave him the lowdown on the situation.

Jake eyed the hotel speculatively. "So she spent the entire night in her hotel room? Alone?"

He sounded disappointed.

"Her lights were on for most of the night. But I haven't seen much movement this past while. Maybe she finally fell asleep."

"What is she doing in there?" Jake asked.

Pierce handed Jake the video camera, then clapped him on the shoulder. "Don't fall asleep and maybe you'll find out."

He returned to his car, a nondescript brown Nissan. The Nissan was perfect for surveillance jobs like this one—no one ever seemed to notice his vehicle, or remember what it looked like. After starting the engine he headed in the general direction of home—a loft in one of the old warehouses on the eastern shore of Lake Union. His apartment was across the hall from his business address, a handy arrangement that suited him fine. Both places had been decorated with a modern, sparse sensibility. Muted colors, very ergonomic.

Cass would have hated it.

After they were married, they'd bought a town house. She'd decorated it top to bottom with furniture that belonged in another century and lots of area rugs with neatly combed fringes. Her hobby had been needlework and she'd filled their walls with framed samplers and their couch and chairs with stiff pillows that God forbid he should ever put his head on.

He'd never felt comfortable in the two-story town house. But he credited Cass for trying. She'd wanted nothing more than to make him a home.

And look where that had gotten her.

He pressed the fingers of one hand to his temple. He couldn't think about that now. Best to think of nothing, to *feel* nothing.

For the third time that night, he raised the volume on the car radio. Then he drove right by the turn that would have taken him home. He kept driving, aimlessly, lost in the sweet nirvana of a passionate woman's voice on a cold winter night.

"IT WOULDN'T BE *Seattle after Midnight* if we didn't play a little Coltrane," Georgia said.

There were only ten minutes left in her show. Pierce had ended up parking on the shore of Lake Union. Now he wondered why he'd felt the need to seek out water when there was so much of the damn stuff in the air tonight. He'd lived in Seattle almost half his life, but every winter it always seemed like he'd never see the sun again.

"Michael Harper had this to say about John Coltrane. *You pick up the horn with some will and blow into the freezing night.* That's what we need tonight, don't you think? A little tenor love…"

Georgia's husky voice faded as Coltrane's saxophone expanded into the nighttime airwaves. A sweet melancholy stole over Pierce, and he wondered, with something bordering awe, how she did it. How did this Georgia woman combine words and music, poetry and her simple stories, in such a way that she made him feel as if he were alive again?

How many other people in Seattle were listening right now? Men and women working the nightshift, insomniacs, the brokenhearted. Did they all feel the way he did—as if Georgia was speaking directly to them, her honeyed voice meant for only their ears?

The song ended and there was a momentary silence before Georgia spoke again. Actually she sighed. "Amazing, isn't he? I have one more song to end our journey through this night, but first let's take another caller. Hello, this is Georgia and you're on *Seattle after Midnight*." She paused. "Is anyone there?"

"Georgia?"

"This is Georgia. Who am I speaking to?"

"Um…Jack."

"Hi, Jack. Did you want to request a song tonight?"

"Not really. I just wanted to talk to someone. I listen to you every night. Sometimes I imagine we're in the same room, like friends or something."

"That's sweet. I'm glad you like the show."

"I love the show. And I liked the songs you played tonight. They're kind of, well, *old*...but powerful, too."

"That's the magic of the minor key. And I have another for you tonight, Seattle. This collaboration between Billy Joel and Ray Charles will make you wish you had a baby grand in your life."

Pierce anticipated the song before it began, and when the soulful opening chords reached his ears, he felt again the aching longing that this show seemed to awaken in him.

Slowly he cruised the length of Fairview Avenue, wondering about the guy who'd made that last call. What would incite someone to pick up the phone and to talk to a woman he'd never met—a woman who wouldn't know him from Adam if she passed him on the street—and tell her things he probably wouldn't tell his closest friend?

The ten-digit number sprang to his mind again. The weight of his cell phone in the breast pocket of his jacket suddenly seemed unbearably tempting. To think that all he had to do was punch some numbers with his finger and he would be able to talk to her...

Jeez. He *was* going crazy. Why couldn't he stop fantasizing about someone he'd never met? He wasn't *that* lonely.

Or maybe he was. He stopped his car, realizing that by subconscious design he'd ended up outside the office complex that housed KXPG Radio. The five-story brick building had a parking lot on one side and a coffee shop next to that. Across the street the still waters of Lake Union seemed like nothing but a silent, black pit.

What was he doing here? Hoping to catch a glimpse of Georgia as she left the building for the night?

Pathetic, he thought, but he kept his car parked right where it was, at a meter on the deserted street. Every night he felt as if she were speaking directly to him, when in fact she was reaching out to thousands. They'd never met; he was nuts to believe any sort of connection existed between them.

"Well, that's our show for tonight, Seattle. Wait, I see I have another call from Jack. Are you still there?"

"I'm here, Georgia. I wanted to say that I really liked that song. Can't you play just one more tune?"

"I'm sorry, but we're out of time tonight—"

"Well, is it possible to see you after the show?"

For the first time that night, possibly all day, Pierce smiled. The guy had nerve, at least.

"After the show there is no more Georgia. Like Cinderella's stagecoach, I turn into a pumpkin. Come again tomorrow, Seattle. When the midnight hour strikes, you'll know where to find me."

Georgia shared a final bit of poetry before sign-ing off. Pierce had no interest in the radio after that, preferring silence to the insipid programming that followed *Seattle after Midnight.*

He leaned his head against the seat rest, his eyes burning from fatigue. Logic told him to start his car and go home. But he didn't. He eyed the outdoor parking lot next to the KXPG office tower and won-dered which of the handful of vehicles sitting there at five in the morning might belong to Georgia.

Not one of the cars seemed to fit. The dark sedan was too conservative, the lemon-colored VW too bubbly…

Oh, for Pete sake. Just go home, would you?

He didn't. And fifteen minutes later his tenacity was rewarded as a woman, who could only be Geor-gia, dashed out of the building.

She wore a knee-length trench coat and held something that might have been a briefcase over her head to protect her hair from the rain. She was shorter than he'd imagined. And slightly more rounded, but it was hard to tell for sure with that bulky coat. In the glare of an outdoor streetlamp, her hair glowed like soft gold.

The security guard had held the outer door open for her and continued to watch after her as she raced for her car. Pierce opened his window in time to hear her call out, "Thanks, Monty. I'm fine—really."

The security guard waved, then returned to his post inside the building. No sooner had the door swung shut behind him, than Georgia let out a scream.

CHAPTER TWO

GEORGIA LAMONT felt like a fool for screaming. It was only a rose tucked into the handle of her car, but when her fingers had closed over it, she'd felt one of the thorns dig deep into her thumb. She supposed she'd already been a little emotionally sensitive thanks to that last caller.

Over the years she'd been in this business, both here and in South Dakota, she'd developed a sixth sense about the people who phoned in to talk to her. She could tell when someone was a bit off, or had been drinking, or was just the obnoxious sort. But Jack tugged at her heartstrings. She intuited deep sorrow in him. Too much sorrow for someone so young.

Georgia brought her injured thumb to her mouth and tasted blood, then froze at the sound of footsteps slapping on pavement, moving fast, moving *closer.*

A quick glance toward the street revealed a tall man in dark clothes running toward her. He didn't seem to care about the rain, which drizzled down his hair and face, unchecked.

She thought of screaming again. But the building's security guard would never hear her out here. No time to unlock the door and scramble inside her car—she'd have to face him….

The man, as if sensing her fear, stopped a good ten feet away from her. "Are you okay? I heard you scream."

He was coming to save her. Not attack her. Fear turned to relief, then to intrigue. Who was he? What was he doing here?

"I'm fine, thanks. Just cut my finger." She nodded toward her door, where the rose was still jammed under the handle.

He stared at her a moment, then smiled. "Sorry. That voice. It's just strange to hear you in person."

He had an attractive smile, but there was a bleakness in his eyes that suggested he didn't use it often. "Do you listen to my show?"

She wondered what he was doing out on the streets of Seattle at this time of night…actually, morning. Something about the way he carried his body made her think he might be a cop, but she'd seen the car he'd sprinted from and it wasn't a patrol car.

"I listen most nights," he said.

Lots of people told her this, and she always felt complimented. But this man's confession gave her a different, much more unsettling reaction.

Ignoring her throbbing thumb, she held out her hand. "I'm Georgia Lamont."

"Pierce Harding." He stepped closer, took her hand tenderly and let it go almost immediately. "I see you're juggling a few things. Can I help you into your car?"

When she hesitated, he dug a business card out of his wallet. "I'm a private investigator," he said. "I was just on my way home from an assignment, when I happened to hear your scream."

How had he heard her scream from his car? Surely his window hadn't been open in the rain? She tucked his card into the pocket of her trench coat and looked at him thoughtfully.

He was still maintaining a respectable distance, his manner completely nonthreatening. He was also slowly, but surely, becoming drenched. As was she.

She turned back to the car door and that silly flower jammed in the handle.

"Should I remove that for you?" Pierce Harding offered again.

She nodded. "Thanks, that would be great."

It took him only a moment. The thorns seemed to have no effect on him.

He looked up at her with surprise on his face. "There's a note."

"Really?" She hadn't seen anything earlier.

He unraveled something from the stem, then handed her a piece of paper, punctured in one place by a thorn. Then he removed the keys from her hand and unlocked the door and held it open. With the added light from the interior of her car, she could read the message easily.

Georgia—A dozen roses…then you'll be mine.

"Oh, my." She thought of the guy who'd called her tonight. Jack. He'd asked to see her after her show. Was this from him?

"From your boyfriend?" Pierce asked the question casually, but his dark eyes narrowed as he waited for her response.

She didn't have a boyfriend, but she wouldn't tell him that. Not yet, anyway. There was something very attractive, almost compelling, about this man. But he was, after all, a virtual stranger.

"This is probably from one of my listeners. Kind of sweet of him to come out in all this rain," she said, trying to convince herself that it was, that there was nothing sinister in the phrase *then you'll be mine*.

Pierce Harding brushed a sheen of water from his face. "Seems a little suspect to me. How do you think he knew which car was yours?"

"A lucky guess?" It occurred to her that for all she knew, the rose had been left by this very man in front of her. In fact, he could be the guy who'd called himself Jack.

But no. Jack had sounded young and insecure, nothing like this self-assured stranger.

"Maybe," Pierce allowed. He stepped aside and gestured for her to get into the car. After a brief hesitation, that's what she did, dropping her case to the passenger seat, along with the rose and the note.

Pierce leaned inside to pass her the keys. His hand was wet and cold, just like hers. She smiled up at him briefly, uncertainly.

"You're soaked," he said. "You'd better get going. Drive carefully, Ms. Lamont."

He stood back for her to close the door, but she didn't. Instead she peered up at him. He looked even taller from this vantage point. She noted his long, lean legs, and broad, powerful shoulders. If he'd intended to hurt her, he could have done so long ago.

Besides, she was new in town and working nights made it difficult to meet people. How was she going to broaden her horizons if she wasn't willing to take the odd chance or two?

One thing she knew for sure. If she drove off now, she would never see Pierce Harding again. Somehow she couldn't stand the thought of that.

This man was strong, capable, attractive…in a craggy sort of way. But it was the hint of sadness in the tired lines that bracketed his mouth that tugged at her heart.

In him she saw a different sadness than the one she'd sensed in Jack. A wiser, deeper, more pervasive sort of sadness.

"Is something wrong, Georgia?"

He hadn't called her Ms. Lamont this time, she noticed. "I was just wondering…I don't mean to be forward, this is strictly a friendly offer. But could I buy you a cup of coffee? For coming to my aid and everything? The coffee shop next door is open twenty-four hours."

Pierce Harding looked surprised at first, which of course he would be. Women weren't supposed to do things like invite strange men for coffee. Especially men who stepped out of dark shadows at the suspiciously right moment.

But no way could this man be the same guy who'd called her station and left her the rose. Every instinct Georgia possessed told her that was impossible.

"I'd be glad to join you for a coffee." He glanced across the parking lot to the café she'd indicated. "Want to make a run for it?"

"Why not? We're already soaked as it is."

He held out his hand and she didn't hesitate to take it. If all went well, soon she'd know much more about this man than just his name. And if things clicked between them, she might even end up with a date.

GEORGIA TOOK her bottle of orange juice and carrot muffin to a booth in the far corner. Pierce followed with his mug of coffee.

At the till, he'd tried to pay but she'd insisted she owed him.

For what, he wasn't sure. Saving her from a thorny rose?

He slid onto the bench seat across from her, watching covertly as she unscrewed the lid on the bottle of juice, then inserted two skinny straws. He couldn't believe he was really sitting here, with Georgia from KXPG, watching her sipping juice and breaking away pieces of her super-size muffin to pop into her mouth. Her hair hung in damp curls around a heart-shaped face.

Sweet, he thought. *She looks like a really sweet person.* Not exactly the image he'd attributed to her from listening to her show. But captivating none the less.

"I'm always starving after a show. I think it's the crash after my adrenaline rush, you know?"

He nodded, fascinated suddenly by her eyes, which were open and honest, a vibrant blue. Not what he'd imagined, at all.

"Where are you from?"

"Seattle?" She offered hesitantly.

"With that accent? No way." Funny how her slight twang didn't come across on her radio program.

"You're right." She gave a resigned shrug of her shoulders. "I grew up on a farm in South Dakota. I went to college in Minnesota, then got my first job at an oldies station in Brookings. From there I moved to classic rock in Sioux Falls."

"How did you end up in Seattle?"

"Pure luck. The program director for KXPG happened to stop at a motel in Sioux Falls while on vacation with his kids last August. I guess his wife had just left him and he and the kids had taken off on an impromptu road trip. Anyway, the night they were in Sioux Falls, his youngest turned sick with the flu. Mark said listening to my program helped both of them get through that night. The very next day I had a job offer."

"I'm not surprised it only took one show to impress him."

"Well, thanks. But what about you? Pierce. That's an unusual name. Where did it come from?"

"God only knows. Maybe the doctor who delivered me?" He definitely could not imagine his mother pouring over baby name books, the way Cass had done. And Cass hadn't even been pregnant. Just dreaming…

The memory pricked at his old stockpile of regrets and Pierce put his hand to his temple.

From across the table, Georgia clearly waited for more details about his life. She was probably curious about all the usual things. Where he'd grown up, gone to school, all that crap. In the end, though, she asked just one question.

"Were you a cop before you became an investigator?"

Now that was a perceptive question. Not that he should be surprised to find Georgia Lamont perceptive. Wasn't that the very quality that drew him to her show every evening?

Georgia gave the impression that she understood all the worst pain and sorrow that could befall a human being. And yet, now that he'd met her, he'd guess that she'd experienced very little, or none, of the seamier side of life herself.

Likable, honest, wholesome…those were the adjectives that summed up the real Georgia Lamont. So how did she reach out to the lonely and disenfranchised the way she did? Who was that worldly, sultry enchantress she projected on air?

"I was." His days as a cop seemed like a lifetime ago. "But I started my own business a couple of years ago. Mostly, it's not a bad way to earn a living."

"Tell me about some of your cases."

"I don't solve a murder every week," he warned her, having come across this misconception more than a few times. "In fact, I don't even own a gun. A lot of my work involves tracking witnesses, locating debtors, uncovering insurance fraud, background checks."

"I always imagine private investigators following cheating spouses around. Do you handle those sorts of cases, too?"

"That's not my favorite line of work. But occasionally I take on something like that."

"Is that what you were doing tonight?"

He paused, then admitted as much with a nod. "My client had to go out of town on business. He was worried his wife was planning to meet with another man while he was gone."

"And was he right?"

"I'm not sure. His wife took off for a hotel as soon as he left. She's still there now. But as far as I can tell, she's alone in that room. I figure her lover must have stood her up."

"But then why not return home?"

"Exactly."

"Hmm. That's an interesting puzzle." Georgia put one elbow on the table, then rested her chin in her hand. "Maybe she's a spy. Maybe she's planning to sell corporate secrets to someone else at the hotel."

He tried to picture well-dressed, sophisticated Jodi Calder as a spy. Couldn't do it.

"Tell me the truth," Georgia asked suddenly. "Did you really just happen to be driving by when you heard me scream?"

Oh, hell. He wished he could say he had. He let himself study her for a few moments, as he admitted to himself that his preoccupation with her definitely had a sexual edge. She hadn't said anything when he'd suggested the rose had come from a boyfriend, but he guessed that she was currently available. She didn't wear a ring on her fourth finger of her left hand, at least.

"Sorta. Not really."

She waited and he felt even more of a fool. He was

going to sound like a groupie, as bad as that fellow who'd left the rose on her car.

"I had just finished my surveillance shift on that case I was telling you about. I'd been listening to your show and so I knew it was over and that you'd be leaving the building soon. The KXPG office building is right on my way home. When I reached it—I stopped. I can't explain why I did that. I don't make a habit of things like this…."

"It's okay." She seemed amused, not annoyed or put out by his explanation.

"I must sound like an idiot."

"Not at all. It's a compliment, isn't it? That you liked my show enough to wonder about me."

"You must get guys bugging you all the time."

"It is an occupational hazard," she admitted. "Usually they stick to phone calls though."

He wished this latest creep had done the same. Only then, he would never have met Georgia. "Would you mind if I took another look at the note that was attached to the rose?"

She opened her bag and fished out the piece of paper. He flattened it on the table and read out loud, "'A dozen roses…then you'll be mine.'"

"Kind of weird, huh?"

"Why does he mention a dozen roses, when he only gave you one?"

"No idea."

Pierce turned the paper over, checking to see if

he'd missed anything. There were no clues that he could spot. The note had been typed on a laser quality printer, using standard issue paper.

"I had a guy phone the show a couple of times tonight. He was sweet and sounded lonely. I'll bet he left the rose for me."

"Jack?"

She nodded.

"I heard his calls. He sounded young and insecure. The guy who wrote this note is all too sure of himself. Notice, he isn't *asking* if you'll be his. He's *telling* you."

A little furrow formed between the pale lines of her eyebrows. "Do you think I should be worried? I've had listeners leave me presents before. One woman in Sioux Falls used to bake me a Christmas cake every December."

"Lucky you."

She laughed. "I didn't actually eat it, I confess."

Pierce wrapped his hands around the warm mug of coffee that he was making a point not to drink. He was going to have a difficult enough time falling asleep as it was. Georgia put out this energy… He could feel himself feeding off it. And not just in a sexual way, although there was that, too.

"Any idea how he would know which car was yours?" he asked, as he'd asked her earlier out in the parking lot. He, himself, had been surprised to discover the yellow VW belonged to Georgia. Though now that he'd talked to her face-to-face, he could see that it fit.

From his quick glance over the vehicle, though, he'd spotted nothing to give away the fact that the car was hers, other than a smear of lipstick on the KXPG commuter mug in her cup holder. Which matched exactly the shade of lipstick she was wearing right now. "Maybe he's seen you drive to work."

"Which would mean he's been watching me." Georgia shivered, then neatly folded the paper liner which had held her muffin. "I don't like the idea of that."

"From now on you should get the security guard at KXPG to walk you right to your car. No more watching from an open door."

"Jack left me a rose. Not a bomb threat."

"A little caution wouldn't hurt. At home, too. Has this guy ever tried to contact you there?"

She shook her head. "No. And my phone is unlisted. I've always done that because as a jock, you do run across these crazies now and then. Usually they make annoying calls for a few weeks, then give up."

But this guy had made personal contact through the rose. Pierce wished Georgia were a little more concerned than she appeared to be. He dug into the pocket of his jeans for another business card. The one he'd given her earlier had probably turned to mush from the rain.

"Here. If he sends you anything else, let me know, okay? You should probably call the police, too, Georgia. Just to be on the safe side."

"The police?"

From her incredulous tone, he could tell she was unlikely to take his advice. She gazed at his card for several seconds, then tucked it into her cavernous black leather bag.

"Thank you again for everything. It's nice to know that, even in a big city like Seattle, people are willing to help strangers."

Her comment reminded him that though he felt like he knew her very well, the first she'd ever heard of him was tonight. "You're welcome, Georgia."

There was a moment of silence, while he considered the possibility of asking her out. She seemed as if she were waiting for him to do just that. She was new to Seattle, and *she'd* asked *him* for the coffee. He could tell by the way she looked at him that she liked what she saw.

Which only proved how fallible she was. If she could see him on the inside, she'd know better than to get too close. If she knew what had happened to Cass...

His wife had been a sweetheart and he could tell Georgia was from the same mold. Those kinds of women needed to be protected from men like him. No matter how much her radio persona attracted him, the real Georgia was much too vulnerable and innocent. A small-town girl. A good girl.

Let her stay that way, he cautioned himself. Let her find a nice guy who wants to settle down and raise a family. That's what women like Georgia—and Cass—wanted and deserved.

"Are you okay to drive home alone?" he asked.

He could tell that wasn't what she'd been hoping he would say. After a slight pause, she drew back. "I'll be fine."

He wasn't surprised when she cleaned up after herself, putting the bottle in a container for recyclables, then trashing the muffin liner and napkin. He rose from his seat, leaving his coffee cup on the table and walked her to her car.

It was still drizzling. And dark. The interior clock on her dash told him it was almost 6:30 a.m.

"Nice meeting you, Georgia."

She slipped behind the steering wheel. "You, too." She gave him one last look and he could see her uncertainty. She'd undoubtedly sensed his attraction to her, just as he'd picked up on hers to him. She had to be wondering why he wasn't asking to see her again.

If only she could know how lucky she was that this was ending right here.

GEORGIA HAD NEVER met a man like Pierce Harding. Definitely not in South Dakota, and not in Seattle, either. There was something hard about him, as well as sad. A man of mystery and secrets. His face was arresting—lean and sculpted, with dark eyes that flashed with intuitive intelligence. The way he held his powerful body, so contained and yet with such presence, made her suspect that he was a man who never fully relaxed.

She was so curious about him. Usually she found it easy to get people to open up to her. That was one of her gifts. But she'd never encountered anyone as reserved as Pierce. Despite having spent almost an hour with him over coffee, she still knew next to nothing about him.

Like, did he have a girlfriend? She hadn't had the nerve to ask. Bad enough that she'd invited him for coffee—she'd never made the first move on a guy before. Even though she'd disguised her offer as a gesture of thanks, she suspected he'd seen right through her.

He was just the kind of guy who would.

Had he guessed how badly she'd wanted him to ask her out? She'd lingered at the booth hoping he would say something. But he hadn't, and she didn't think it was because he was shy.

Georgia parked her car in the lane next to her side of her rented two-story duplex. The windows on both halves of the building were dark. Obviously her neighbor, Fred Sorenson, a retired postal worker, was still sleeping. She checked his door to make sure it was locked and found it open. Sighing, she used her spare copy of his key to secure the deadbolt.

Though he was only in his early seventies, Fred could be forgetful at times. He also had trouble with his knees and sometimes spent the entire night on the sofa rather than deal with the stairs to the upper level bedrooms.

Once she'd suggested he might be more comfortable in a bungalow, or perhaps a condominium. He'd simply shaken his head. Belmont Avenue had been home to him for decades. He and his wife had raised their daughter in this very duplex. Though his wife had died two years ago, and his daughter was married and living in Australia, he still wouldn't move.

Georgia stepped over the two-foot hedge that separated their properties. A puddle of water had pooled on the wooden step up to her porch. She splashed through it, then searched for her own house key on her ring.

Inside, the dark hall did not feel welcoming. She dropped her bag onto the wooden bench, then shrugged out of her wet jacket and hung it on a peg near the door.

She flicked on the hallway light and climbed the stairs. She hesitated, then reached into the bag to pull out Pierce Harding's business card. In her bedroom, she switched on a lamp, then sat on her bed. She liked that it was a no-frills card, sensible and somehow manly, too. She wished she could believe that he'd handed it to her because he wanted to hear from her again. But when she remembered his vaguely aloof farewell, she knew that explanation wasn't likely. He'd offered his card as a courtesy, in case that flower turned out not to be an innocent gift after all. In fact, he may have intended for her to consider hiring his services.

She felt her face grow hot with belated embarrassment. Of course, that was what he'd intended. She dropped the card into the wastepaper basket, disgusted with herself for feeling so disappointed.

She'd only just met him. Why should she care if he'd been courting her business, rather than her?

WHAT A NIGHT.

At two in the afternoon, Georgia pulled herself out of the warm covers and sat on the side of the bed, her feet flat on the cold hardwood floor. She hadn't slept well at all, unable to stop thinking about the man she'd met last night.

Had Pierce Harding really been as incredible as she remembered? In the cold light of day, it didn't seem possible. Her mother had always said her unrealistic romantic streak would cause trouble for her one day. Falling for a dark, intriguing stranger who had rushed to her rescue fit in with that theory all right.

Georgia glanced at the rose. She'd left it on her dresser and it was drooping sadly, the petals blackened along the edges. Poor Jack. He'd gone to all that effort and she hadn't even bothered to put the blossom in water.

Well, it was too late now. She dropped the rose into the wastepaper basket, then froze, as Pierce's business card caught her eye.

Oh, heck, maybe she should keep it. Just in case.

She placed the card on her dresser, and began to plan her day. She'd buy groceries first, then put together several home-cooked meals for Fred's freezer. Since she loved spending time in the kitchen, Georgia didn't consider this a chore but something to look forward to.

An hour later, after marking three recipes and compiling a substantial grocery list, Georgia was at the front door, making sure she had money, the list and her keys. She glanced in the mirror above the painted wooden bench to check her lipstick, then opened the door.

Something on the porch floor caught her eye.

It was a rose. Another red rose.

She glanced around the neighborhood looking for something or someone who didn't belong. But all was quiet and still. She stepped out onto the porch to check the blind spot behind the rattan chair and footstool she kept out here. Again, nothing was amiss.

Whoever had left her this rose was long gone. Georgia stooped and grasped the end of the stem, careful not to prick herself on the thorns this time.

Like before, a note had been wrapped around the stem. She went inside, closing the door and locking it, before she scanned the short missive.

Georgia, the typed message read. *I heard the song you played for me last night. Did you know I was listening? Have you seen me watching you, too?*

She frowned, trying to temper her rising anxiety. She had to stay calm. Think clearly. This *had* to be from Jack. She'd played a song for him last night. Of course, she'd known he'd been listening. But watching?

He must have followed her home. She shivered at the idea, then shoved the note into her bag. What should she do?

The image of Pierce's business card came immediately to mind. He'd said to call if she had any problems. Was this second rose a problem?

Judging by the pounding of her heart and the sweating of her palms, it was.

CHAPTER THREE

PIERCE'S OFFICE space consisted of three intercon-
nected rooms. One was his, another was shared by
Jake Jeffrey and Will Livingstone and the third was
for storage and reference materials. He had a computer with Internet access set up in there that he and
his staff all shared.

The receptionist, Robin Housley, sat in the cross-
roads of the three offices. She had a computer that
was supposed to be used to keep track of appoint-
ments and addresses and the bookkeeping records.
Unfortunately Robin had no experience with even the
most basic of computer accounting packages. She
kept a manual ledger and was forever scribbling numbers on odd scraps of paper, which she stuck to the
computer monitor. At least it was useful for something.

When she'd applied for the job of receptionist at
Harding Investigations she'd stood in front of his
desk and said, "I'm forty-seven and completely un-
trained for any type of job. My husband left me five
days ago and I have an autistic child to provide for."

It was quite the job résumé. He'd never heard another like it.

Unless it was Jake's, the kid he'd hired as a general gofer and legman who came to him initially with his ankle in a cast. Or Will Livingstone, who'd been "retired" from his job with a bigger agency, but who couldn't afford to stop working just because he was over sixty.

When he'd started his agency after Cass's death, Pierce hadn't intended to have one employee, let alone a staff. The point of leaving police work had been to work alone.

But his business had grown so quickly—mostly thanks to references from the cops he used to work with—that he'd been forced to hire. Now Pierce was happiest when his employees were doing the jobs he'd employed them to do without asking any questions or needing any help. That wasn't often.

And then there was the cat.

Entering his office now, Pierce could see her curled in the top drawer of his filing cabinet. She'd claimed the space the first day she'd shown up, mewing at his door. He'd given her to Robin, instructing her to get rid of the damn pest.

An hour later, he'd spotted the stray drinking milk from his coffee mug. "What's this cat still doing here?" he'd demanded of Robin.

"Ask her," Robin had shrugged. "She won't talk to me."

And, though she never did talk to Pierce, either, she did seem to like him best, sleeping in his office, curling up on his lap whenever he sat still for more than five minutes, mewing when he first came in for the day.

She did that now, standing up, arching her back, stretching out her front paws.

"Yeah, yeah," he muttered back at her, heading straight for his desk. Robin was on his heels.

"Do you have the time sheets from last week for me yet?"

"I do." From his briefcase he pulled out the paperwork he'd finished earlier, knowing Robin would be drafting the invoices this afternoon. There would be errors, and he'd have to correct them, but that was the way things went around here.

Robin took the information from him, handing him a cup of coffee in exchange. When she'd first started, he'd told her she didn't need to do that, wait on him like some kind of servant. But making coffee was the one thing she was really good at and so he hadn't tried too hard to dissuade her.

"Thanks." He took his first sip, only then feeling that he might be able to get through the rest of this day after all.

"You have a three o'clock appointment," Robin told him. "A new client."

He frowned. With around-the-clock surveillance on the Calder case right now, everyone was pretty busy. And he'd been planning to spend his afternoon in the courthouse, digging through land files for one of his lawyer clients.

"Hard to say over the phone, but she sounded young. And sexy."

He raised his eyebrows at Robin, not changing his expression in any other way.

"I'll start a file for her. Leave it on your desk." Robin left his office, not bothering to close the door, which was just as well, since she was typically in and out so often there was little point in erecting a barrier between them.

He'd assign Jake the courtroom job, he decided, reaching for the phone.

An hour later, Georgia Lamont swept into his office in a red leather jacket, well-fitted jeans, and high-heeled boots.

"Told you she was sexy," Robin hissed at him, just before she admitted the woman into his office. "And she brought you a flower!"

GEORGIA FELT some trepidation as the middle-aged receptionist closed the door behind her. She set the rose on Pierce's desk, then sat, uninvited, in the chair obviously meant for clients.

She'd never hired an investigator before. And, though they'd shared a coffee, Pierce looked at her with all the warmth of a perfect stranger.

As their gazes met and held, she had the urge to run

out of the room. What was she doing here? She'd been given a rose—how threatening was that? Oh, sure she'd been startled at first. But she wasn't really scared of the poor soul who had taken the time to leave her what he probably thought was a nice surprise.

She felt herself blush as she acknowledged the real reason she'd made this appointment. To see Pierce again.

She felt suddenly sure that he knew exactly why she was here and why she'd dressed the way she had—in the sexiest outfit she owned.

Without speaking, he picked up the rose and the note that she'd set down with it. While he studied the short message, she glanced around his office. It was a modern, utilitarian space, with taupe carpeting and natural, light maple furniture. In the corner, a well-worn leather chair looked like a good spot to sit and read.

Framed on the off-white walls was his state license. His bookshelves were crammed, mostly with phone books from various American cities and a few Canadian ones besides.

"I didn't expect you to have a receptionist." This was a real business. She'd pictured him on his own, in a dusty, paper-strewn room with a window-fronted door. He should have had his feet up on his desk when she'd entered. And a cigarette in his mouth.

That's what she got for watching too many movies. Preconceptions, of the extremely romantic sort.

"When did you get this?"

Pierce looked grouchy. Or maybe he was just tired. They'd been up late last night and he probably hadn't had the luxury of sleeping until early afternoon as she had.

"I found it on my porch this afternoon. I was stepping out for groceries." Which she still had to do on her way home from this meeting.

"*I heard the song you played for me last night...* Do you know which song he meant?"

"As usual, I played several requests. Including one for Jack."

"You still think the roses are coming from him?"

"Doesn't that seem most likely?"

He ignored her, as he focused on the next part of the message. "This stuff about watching you..." He lifted his head again. "Can't say I like the sound of that."

"No."

"Have you noticed anyone hanging around your home? Tailing you in your car?"

"Not at all. But he must have followed me home last night."

"Possibly. Or he already knew where you lived from trailing you on a different night."

"Most stalkers don't turn out to be violent," she said, more to convince herself than Pierce.

"Maybe so. But you really should call the police just in case. And install a security system in your home. Unless you already have one?"

She shook her head.

Pierce opened a file labeled with her name and started writing on the first page. Then he jotted a note on a pad by his phone. "I'll get back to you."

"On the security system?"

"Yeah. I might be able to pick up something wholesale." He focused his dark eyes on her. "A good security system, a little extra caution on your part and a precautionary phone call to the police should be enough for now. Unless you want me to put some time into tracking this guy down?"

"Oh, no. That's not necessary. I just wanted your opinion. About whether this was something to be worried about. I'm willing to pay for your time, of course."

For the first time a smile crept up one side of his mouth. "I'm not going to charge you for advising you to be careful. As for the security system, I don't recommend anything fancy, just an alarm so you'll know if someone tries to tamper with your windows or doors. Usually the sound of the buzzer is enough to frighten an intruder away. Do your neighbors live close?"

She thought of Fred, only a wall away. "Oh, definitely."

"Good, then I think that's all you need."

"And the cost of the security system?"

"I'm not sure, but the parts are not expensive. Especially when you consider the value of your own peace of mind."

He capped his pen and set it on the desk. Closed her file. But not, she noticed, before inserting the two notes she'd given him earlier.

"What about installation?"

"I'll take care of it."

Given his cool demeanor, she was surprised by the offer. "I can't let you do that."

"Why not?"

Wasn't it obvious? "You're running a business. You can't give your services away for free."

"Let me worry about my business. I haven't missed a payroll yet."

She heard the tinge of irony in his tone and guessed his business was actually doing very well. A fact supported by the clean, polished look of his offices.

"It just seems odd you would do this favor for someone you only met last night."

"Actually, Georgia, I met you more than a month ago. It's *you* who only met *me* last night. Let's just say I want to ensure the continued success of *Seattle after Midnight.*"

WITH A PROMISE to stop by later that evening to install the security system, Pierce walked Georgia to the door, past Robin who didn't even try to pretend she wasn't interested in their conversation.

As soon as Georgia was gone, he handed Robin the file. "Put this away, please."

Robin took a peek inside. "She didn't sign the contract. Did you get a retainer?"

"I did not," he said in a tone meant to discourage further questions.

"I see. She's a friend, then."

"She isn't a friend."

"An admirer?"

"Robin…"

"Would you like me to put your rose in a vase?"

He retreated behind his office door, closing it firmly between them.

GEORGIA STOPPED at the IGA to pick up her groceries, then went home to cook. She was relieved to find no roses waiting for her when she returned and gave herself over to the double pleasure of cooking and listening to Vivaldi for a change.

She was spooning chicken cacciatore—her mother's recipe—into individual serving containers when her doorbell rang. She wiped her hands on a towel then went to see who was there.

Pierce stood on her welcome mat, a large cardboard box in hand.

Her heart thumped at the sight of him. He was dressed as he'd been in the office that day, in jeans and a black shirt made out of cotton so fine it looked as soft as silk. He wiped his feet on the mat several times before stepping inside. It wasn't raining, but the evening sky was dreary.

"I didn't expect you so soon." She sounded breathless, not at all like herself. But Pierce didn't seem to notice—not her voice or anything else about her, either.

He settled into work right away, and after watching him for a while, she returned to the kitchen. She checked on the beef stew simmering on the stove, then made a batch of cheese biscuits. When those were ready, she labeled several packages for Fred and placed them in a cardboard box.

Pierce was in the entry, installing a motion detector in the corner of the hall.

"I'm going to take this over to my next-door neighbor, Fred."

"I saw him on the porch when I came in. Seems like the kind of guy who likes to keep an eye on things."

"That's Fred all right." He'd been like a mother hen since she'd moved in. Warning her about the dangers of the big city and the need for a pretty, young woman to be careful. Meanwhile, he went to sleep with his front door unlocked at night.

Chuckling to herself, Georgia stepped over the hedge and found Fred on the porch, as if he were waiting for her.

"Thought I smelled something cooking over there." He gave her a smile and a wink. "What did you make this week, Georgie-girl?"

"Let's go inside and I'll show you."

She spent the better part of an hour talking to Fred, who insisted she share half a beer with him while he ate her stew. She stored the casseroles in his freezer and made him promise he'd eat one every night.

"Toast and cereal are fine for breakfast and lunch, but you need at least one real meal every day."

He patted her hand. "You sound like my daughter."

She knew Fred's daughter could only afford to visit once every three or four years. She usually preferred to visit Seattle in the summer. Which meant Fred spent every Christmas alone. Maybe next year, she'd invite him to South Dakota with her.

"Did the show go well last night?" Fred asked, as she was preparing to leave.

"Pretty good, thanks."

"I'm sorry I missed it."

"That's okay." Fred was not a night owl, but it was sweet the way he always enquired about her show.

She left his house, hopped the hedge, then bounded up the shallow steps of her own porch. The second she opened her front door an obnoxious, unrelenting screeching filled the air.

Georgia shrieked, then covered her ears. Pierce galloped down the stairs, shot her a look of disbelief, then rounded the corner toward the back door where he'd installed the main control panel.

A moment later, Fred limped over, arriving on

her porch just as Pierce managed to disable the alarm.

"I guess it works," she said sheepishly to Pierce when he returned.

"I'd say so." Pierce offered a hand to her neighbor and the two men chatted about the system for a few minutes. Fred seemed pleased that Georgia was taking security seriously.

"This neighborhood isn't as safe as it used to be. Why just the other day I saw a strange man sitting in a car across the street. Seemed like he was casing the block, if you ask me."

"Oh?" Pierce looked interested. "Can you give me a description of this guy?"

"Would if I could, but he was wearing a baseball cap and my eyes aren't as good as they used to be. I tried to run outside to get his license number but my knees were acting up real bad that day."

"Do you remember which day this was?" Pierce asked.

Fred traced back over the past week and finally settled on a day just before the first rose had been delivered.

"If you happen to notice him again, I'd be glad if you'd let me know." Pierce gave Fred one of his business cards. "Now, let me show you both how this new security system works."

Pierce led Georgia and Fred to the kitchen where the control panel had been installed next to the rear entrance. He explained how to activate the system and how to change the four-number code.

"Keep this portable unit by the front door," he told Georgia, handing her a plastic box about the size of a fat TV remote control. "As long as you punch in your code within thirty seconds of opening the front door, the alarm won't go off."

Later, once Fred had returned home, he nodded at Georgia. "Your neighbor made it over here pretty quick for an old guy."

"Fred's one of the good ones." She brushed a dab of flour from her jeans. If only she'd had time to change before Pierce showed up on her doorstep. "What do you think about that man he saw on the street?"

"Could be your guy. Can't say for sure, of course. I hope Fred will call me if he spots him again."

"I'm sure he will. Fred takes it personally if anything bad happens on the block."

"I'm glad he watches out for you."

They ran out of things to say at the same time. After an awkward pause, Pierce busied himself looking everywhere but at her. He gathered his tools and placed them in the cardboard box he'd brought with him. Georgia readied her checkbook, but as he'd already indicated, Pierce let her reimburse him for the cost of materials only, nothing for his time.

"You'll let me repay you with dinner, at least?"

"That's not necessary."

Though she'd been expecting the rejection, she still felt hurt. If he liked her enough to install the security system for no charge, why not stay for dinner, too?

She could guess the answer. Pierce had connected to the radio Georgia, but not the real-life version.

She must have disappointed him by not living up to her airwave image. Not even the red leather coat and the fashion boots she'd been wearing that afternoon in his office had been enough to heat up her small-town-girl image.

"At least take something with you. You can microwave it at home." She offered him the choice of the chicken or the beef and was rewarded with a grin.

"I feel like I'm on an airplane."

"Trust me, my mother's recipes are nothing like the food you get on an airplane."

He held up one hand. "No insult intended."

She ended up giving him plastic containers of both, as well as a bag containing a half-dozen biscuits. At the door he said, "I'm not sure I didn't get the best deal."

"I'm sure you didn't. Thank you." On her salary she could never have afforded the regular cost of a security system.

"The system only works if you activate it." When she didn't reply, he added, "You will activate it, right? Whenever you're home and especially at night."

"Of course."

He looked at her doubtfully, then finally headed for his car. She watched him go with regret. This was it. She really wouldn't see him again. She went back inside to clean the kitchen after her marathon cooking session. Five minutes hadn't passed when she heard something in the hall.

She lifted her head and listened intently. A second later, she heard another creak. Her spine tingled. She tensed, grabbed the handle of her cast-iron frying pan, then whirled around.

Pierce put his hands up to shield his face.

She screamed. "What are you doing?"

"I had a feeling you'd forget to activate the alarm."

"I completely forgot." She'd have to get used to a new routine.

"I went to a lot of work to wire in that system. Don't you think you could humor me and use the thing? Or at least lock the damn door?"

"I'm sorry." Though they'd never locked their house on the farm, since she'd lived alone she'd been conscientious about doing so. Why she'd forgotten today, she couldn't explain.

"I did have another reason for coming back." Pierce's harsh tone softened as he held up the bag of food she'd given to him. "I've changed my mind about dinner. If you're still willing, I'd be glad to share this with you."

CHAPTER FOUR

GEORGIA SET the table with china plates covered in pretty blue flowers. Pierce looked at those plates with dismay. More evidence that Georgia was exactly the sort of woman he'd pegged her as in the KXPG parking lot last night. The sweet hometown type who baked biscuits without a mix and used her grandmother's heirloom china. She was exactly the sort he had no business getting to know, no business encouraging, no business lusting after.

And that was the hell of it. Even though she wasn't at all his type, he was attracted to her.

Just attracted?

Yes, he assured himself. He might not be the smartest man in the world, but he wasn't foolish enough to make the same mistake twice.

"Would you like a glass of wine with dinner? Or would you prefer a beer or water?"

Telling himself wine was too romantic, Pierce choose beer and was surprised when Georgia asked him to get her one from the fridge, as well.

Georgia spooned hearty beef stew into her pretty

dishes. She prepared a quick salad and put it on the table with a basket of biscuits and a dish of soft butter.

"Looks good." His comment could have applied equally to Georgia as it did to the meal. With her coloring—pink cheeks, blue eyes, golden hair—she didn't need makeup or fancy clothes to sparkle. In blue jeans and a sweater the color of spring grass, she topped any runway model he'd ever seen.

"Tell me about South Dakota," he said once they were both seated and eating. Some interesting African music was playing in the background. Georgia had kicked off her slippers and was sitting cross-legged on her chair. He felt much more relaxed than he'd expected.

"What can I say? I grew up on a farm. I can drive a tractor, operate an auger, bake bread from scratch. I liked living in the country, but from the day I toured the local country station with my sixth grade class I've known I wanted to work in radio."

"Moving to Seattle must have been a big step."

"It was. My parents were apprehensive, to say the least. They still are. But my view is that people are people, no matter where they live."

That was true. But also not. To some extent living in a major city changed people. Living in a poor neighborhood rife with gangs, small-time criminals and prostitutes on every corner changed people, too.

"You disagree?" she said, reading his expression correctly.

"My experience is that people are influenced by their environment. Some more than others."

"Did you grow up in Seattle?"

"New York City." But he didn't want to talk about *that.* "This stew is really good. What are these yellow vegetables? They don't taste like potatoes."

"Turnips," she said, not taking her eyes off him. "When did you leave New York?"

"I was little more than a kid." He'd been sixteen and he'd had a plan. He'd saved for a car and the day he qualified for his license, he'd driven off, not stopping until he reached the ocean.

"So tell me more about your life in South Dakota. Did you leave behind a sweetheart when you moved to Seattle?"

Georgia's pink cheeks grew rosier. "How did you know?"

"Women like you always leave behind a sweetheart when they move to the big city. Was he a farmer?"

She laughed. "You know the script, don't you? Craig's family owns a dairy farm two miles from ours. We grew up together. He really is the nicest guy."

"Do you think he's still waiting for you?"

"I hope not. I told him our relationship was over. That I didn't plan on ever coming back."

Pierce heaped his spoon with stew, then paused, eyebrows raised. "Did he offer to move to Seattle with you?"

"Craig could never be happy anywhere but on the farm."

She hadn't answered the question. Did she miss her farmer more than she was willing to admit? To him her smile looked a little sad. "Are you sure you made the right decision? Maybe life in South Dakota had everything you really need. Everything you really want."

Georgia set down her fork, then took a long drink from her beer. When she was done, she wiped her damp mouth with her napkin and fixed him with an uncompromising look. "What are you saying? That I don't belong in a city like Seattle?"

"No—"

"I've got news for you. I'm good on the radio and I intend to have a syndicated program of my own one day. People all across America are going to listen to me and my show won't be called *Seattle after Midnight* then, it'll be *Georgia after Midnight*."

Her passion surprised him. Then he thought about the siren who drew him to the radio every weeknight and realized he shouldn't have been surprised at all.

"I never meant to question your talent."

"What did you mean to question? You know, you're a cynical man, Pierce Harding. I wonder what made you that way." With her elbows on the table, she folded her hands together and rested her chin on the perch. Gazed at his hands. "I see you don't wear a wedding band. Was it a nasty divorce that gave you this bleak view of the world?"

He blinked with surprise. Turned his head very slightly away from her.

"I'm not divorced." He was suddenly very regretful that he hadn't just driven off when he had the chance. "I'm a widower. My wife died two years ago."

GEORGIA COULD HAVE kicked herself for being so thoughtless. "I'm sorry." The apology sprang immediately to her lips. "How tragic. Was she ill?"

She guessed he didn't want to talk about it. Pierce had sidestepped every one of her personal questions last night and today, too. But she felt it would be callous to just let his statement pass without comment.

"She was killed in a car accident."

Pierce's face settled into grim lines that made him look a good five years older than he had earlier that afternoon. That his emotions regarding his wife ran deep, Georgia had no doubt. But she suspected there was more than grief at play.

"I'm sorry," she said again.

Pierce added nothing to that, and she used the pause in their conversation as an opportunity to clear the dishes. A few minutes later when she offered pie and coffee, she wasn't surprised that Pierce declined.

He glanced at his watch. "I really should be getting to work."

"Same surveillance job as last night?"

He nodded.

She watched him shrug into his leather jacket and put on his shoes. What was it like to have a job like his? She imagined sitting in a car late at night, alone, watching other people live their lives, witnessing the very worst that human behavior had to offer.

"Your work must be very lonely."

"At times. On late-night surveillance jobs the hardest part is staying alert."

Yes, she could see how that would be a challenge. "How *do* you keep from falling asleep?"

At first it seemed he wasn't going to answer. He pulled his car keys from his jacket pocket. Stared at them for a moment as if he wasn't sure what to do with them. Just before he left, he glanced over his shoulder at her.

"I listen to you," he said. And then he was gone.

As SOON AS he'd driven away from Georgia's, Pierce powered on his cell phone and called Will Livingstone, currently working the afternoon shift on the Calder job. Pierce's stint wasn't scheduled to begin for another half hour. But he was sure Will wouldn't object if he spelled him early.

"How's it going, Will?"

"The lady went out shopping for a few hours this

afternoon. The rest of the time she's been in that room without any visitors that I can tell." Will sounded mystified by this.

"Still no man on the scene?"

"Not that I can tell. I'm sorry, Pierce. We're not coming up with any answers here."

"This is a strange one, all right."

Will yawned loudly. "You on your way?"

"Be there in fifteen." Water splashed to the sidewalk as Pierce drove through a puddle in the middle of the road. He stopped at a red light where his eyes were drawn to a thirty-foot spruce tree across the street. The owners had strung colored lights about halfway around the tree, then given up. Must have run out of ladder or lights. Whatever the reason, the result looked ridiculous rather than festive. *Waste of bloody electricity.*

There was hardly any traffic and the rain had slowed to a drizzle. He drove as if on autopilot and tried not to think about the house he'd just left, the meal he'd eaten, the woman whose company he'd shared—and enjoyed. A smart man wouldn't have turned back the way he had. After all, he'd made a clean getaway after installing the security system. Who cared if she used it? He'd done his part by putting it in. His conscience was clear.

Five minutes earlier than he'd said on the phone, Pierce steered into the service station across from the hotel and parked next to Will Livingstone's Toyota.

He acknowledged Will's presence with a nod, then dashed into the small convenience store attached to the gas station. He poured himself an extra-large coffee and grabbed a bag of sunflower seeds and a new package of gum.

The kid behind the counter eyed him curiously. "Still staking out that hotel?"

"Another forty-eight hours."

The kid nodded, trying to look as if this were no big deal to him.

Pierce pocketed the seeds, his gum and the change, then carried his coffee outside. Will unrolled his driver-side window.

"Seems like she's here for the night again," Will said. "You could probably go home for a few hours shut-eye and come back in the morning."

"Probably," Pierce acknowledged. But he wouldn't. Will passed him the log they used to record Jodi's movements.

"Thanks." Pierce returned to his car and settled in. He tore open the tab on his coffee and took a sip of the bitter brew. Levering his seat back about ten degrees, he stretched out his legs.

Across the street the Charleston's fairy lights sparkled. He wondered what Jodi was up to right now. Doing drugs? Getting loaded? What? He couldn't imagine anything so bad that a middle-aged woman would leave her comfortable home and book into a hotel all by herself.

He shifted in his seat and thought about the husband. Steven Calder had left a phone message earlier in the afternoon, then again around five, while Pierce had been at Georgia's. Unsurprisingly, Calder had been unable to contact his wife at home.

Pierce knew he should phone the man, but thoughts of Georgia kept distracting him.

Damn that woman. He couldn't stop himself from glancing at the clock on the dashboard and calculating the hours until her program would begin. He wondered if he would feel the same magic now that he'd met her.

He opened the log and reviewed the entries that had been made by Jake, then Will. Jodi Calder's movements while shopping that afternoon had been carefully tracked. She'd gone to a quick-stop grocer, a bookstore and an office supply shop.

Nothing suspicious in any of that.

In fact, there was nothing suspicious about anything Jodi Calder had done since her husband left town. Except for booking into this hotel room.

After an hour of waiting and watching while nothing happened, Pierce decided to do something he'd never tried in a case like this. He was going to knock on her hotel room door and ask her.

I LISTEN TO YOU, Pierce had said. I LISTEN TO YOU. As she prepared for that evening's show in her studio, Georgia couldn't stop the soundtrack in her head from repeating that line. Something in his delivery, in the heat of his eyes when he'd said it, made her knees feel weak and her insides tingle. She had to keep reminding herself that it was her program he was interested in. Not her body.

She pushed away from the desk where she'd been outlining a script and looked up from her control board through the window to the producer's room. Larry Sizemore sat with his back to her, busy with his last-minute preparations, too. They'd had their preshow meeting half an hour ago. As usual, he'd met all her suggestions and ideas with stony acceptance.

She sighed and turned to the computer on her right. She had some phone calls to edit. Only very rarely did she air calls live as she had last night. Usually she worked prerecorded, edited calls carefully into her program.

Looking into her computer screen, a trick of lighting reflected her own image back at her. What she saw made her sigh.

She knew the image she presented on the air differed from the reality. Though she was twenty-eight, she looked at least five years younger. That might be a benefit to her in ten years, but right now she felt hampered, not only by her appearance, but by her background, her inexperience, her small-town naiveté.

She wanted Pierce to act on the attraction she was

almost sure he felt. Not hold himself back the way he'd done tonight.

I listen to you. To you, Georgia, to you.

She wanted him to hold her in his arms and say those words. Then kiss her. And touch her... Eyes closed, she imagined how it would feel, how his arms would circle her waist, how he'd lift her chin with his finger then...

The phone rang, her private line, zapping fantasy into cold reality. Her first hope was that it was Pierce.

"Yes?"

But it was just Monty from the security desk. There'd been a delivery for her—did she want him to bring it up?

"No, I'll be right there." She ran down the double flight of stairs that led to the main foyer. Monty's desk was to the left of the two revolving doors and the regular set of glass doors that led to the street.

Monty Greenfield, in his fifties and a little portly, straightened in his chair, pulling back his shoulders to better fill his stiffly pressed navy uniform. They usually had a couple of short conversations during the course of an evening. He was new here too, having started his job just weeks before she began hers. He'd needed a change of scene after his wife's death, he'd told her. Apparently Nancy had been sick for a long time.

"Here you go, Georgia. Looks like you have an

admirer." He held up a loosely wrapped package, obviously flowers.

Flowers. Georgia hesitated, then stepped forward. Maybe this would turn out to be something else. From someone else.

"Who made the delivery, Monty?"

He shrugged. "Just some courier on a bike."

"Did you notice the name of the company?"

"Sorry, no. Why? Does it matter?"

"Not really, I guess." But if she knew which courier company had made the delivery, she would have been able to track down the name of the sender.

"So who's the admirer?" Monty teased.

"I wish I knew. If I get another delivery, would you mind making a note of who brings it?"

"Sure. No problem, Georgia. Want me to bring you something from the coffee shop later?"

"That would be lovely. Anything but coffee," she reminded him. Though she enjoyed a latte in the morning, her stomach couldn't handle the brew later in the day.

"Sure thing. Say, I liked that 'Day in the Life of a Fool' song you played last night."

"I thought you would." Monty was a real Kenny Rankin fan.

The phone rang then, and Monty put up his hand indicating that he'd talk to her later. "Security," he said, answering the call.

Georgia ran back up the stairs, the faint aroma

from the wrapped flowers filling her with dread. She closed the door to her studio, then unwrapped the lavender paper. As she'd been afraid, she'd been sent roses—three of them this time. The flowers were still tight hard buds. To her overactive imagination, the thorns looked as if they'd been deliberately sharpened.

The attached note, again typed on plain white paper, read *Counting the days, Georgia. Counting the days.*

CHAPTER FIVE

GEORGIA DROPPED THE roses into the trash with shaking hands. After a moment's hesitation, she rescued the note, shoving it into her bag. She couldn't deal with it now, not when she had to be on the air in such a short time.

She glanced at her phone, and wished she could call Pierce. But she couldn't keep running to him with her problems. She'd contact the police later, she decided. Undoubtedly they'd tell her not to worry. That these sorts of things happened to people in the public eye all the time.

She gathered the script she'd been working on for tonight's show, then perused her playlist. She had some more calls to edit and a few e-mails to answer. Dealing with these routine tasks helped settle her nerves.

One minute before her show, Georgia's stomach fluttered again…this time with a familiar combination of anticipation and unease. The thrill of having graduated to a major city radio station still hadn't worn off. Tempering that thrill, though, was the knowledge that at least a couple employees at KXPG wished she'd never been offered the job.

Unfortunately, her producer was one of them.

From the control room, Larry nodded curtly at her as she slipped her headphones back on. She kept her eye on the second hand as it began its final rotation toward the top of the hour.

Ten seconds. Five. Then one. She leaned into the microphone.

"It's after midnight, Seattle. And you know what that means…."

"…YOU'RE SETTLED IN for another cold winter night with Georgia. I've got some music I hope will warm you up. Let's start with 'Fever,' an ultrasmooth, ultrahot version by Canadian crooner Michael Bublé…."

As long as he had his headphones on, Brady Walsh found it easy to lose himself in Georgia's radio program. But the second he removed them, the sound of his mother crying in the next room tore him apart.

Night after night, it was always the same. God, he was starting to hate his father…. Brady blocked that thought. He knew it was evil. He pushed aside the notes he'd been trying to study for his English test tomorrow. He hadn't managed to get through them even once. English was his most difficult subject, but he didn't care about the test. So what if his grades were dropping? His mother hadn't even noticed on his last report card.

Hard to believe that only six months ago his life had been so different. His mother and father had made a big deal about his report card then. They usually went out for dinner, to a nice restaurant, but not so nice they didn't serve steak or hamburgers or something else Brady liked.

His dad would make a toast. Something about his son making him proud. Then his mother would lean over to kiss him, which was embarrassing as hell, but in a way, kind of nice, too.

Those dinners had been a tradition.

But they didn't seem to have any traditions anymore.

Not wanting to think about the old days, not able to stand the raw sound of his mother's misery either, Brady escaped from his room and grabbed the car key from the usual spot by his mother's purse.

He needed to get out. He needed to think.

Driving the streets in his mother's Audi, listening to the radio, he took the usual route to Courtney's and parked across the street. All the windows were dark. He'd never once seen anyone up this late in that house.

Still, he was content to sit in the shadows, comfortable in the Audi's leather seats, listening to the radio. Sometimes he called Georgia just to talk. Sometimes he asked her to play a song for him. Sometimes, the worst times, he just listened.

Today, he felt like talking.

"Hey, Jack, what's new?" Georgia said, when she picked up the line.

He could tell they weren't on the radio, but he knew she would be recording this. And might air it later. Still, in the dark, with his fake name, he felt comfortable confiding in her.

"There's this girl I like at school…."

"What's her name?"

"Courtney."

"Pretty name."

"Yeah. She passed me in the hall today. We were coming from different classes, both headed for science. The hall was jammed and our arms brushed together for a second. I almost couldn't breathe. Am I strange, or something? I mean it was just an accidental touch, but I can't stop thinking about it."

"You're not strange, Jack. Trust me, your reaction was completely normal."

"I just wish I wasn't such a loser. I wish just once she would look at me. Let me know that I'm alive."

"You mean, let you know that *she knows* you're alive. Right?"

He didn't get the distinction. "Whatever. Can you play me a song, Georgia? You pick something you think I'll like."

"Sure, Jack. One of my favorites is coming up next. It's a good song to listen to when it's raining and you're feeling a little blue…."

Brady waited. Sure enough, when the current song ended, Georgia introduced one by Sting. "'Fragile' was redone by Holly Cole and Jesse Cook, but Sting's version is hard to beat."

The music started, and Brady had to admit, it was unbelievably perfect. How did she do that, he wondered. Match his mood to music.

Brady glanced at the time display. It was getting late. He really should head home. With a sigh, he shifted the car into drive and took off in the rain.

It WAS ONE-THIRTY in the morning and Reid was sleeping in bed next to Sylvie. He'd dozed off after they'd made love, and though she knew she ought to wake him so he could return home to his wife, Sylvie couldn't resist keeping him to herself a while longer.

The radio was still playing quietly in the room. *Seattle after Midnight.* An evocative song by Sting ended and Georgia's rich voice came on the air.

"That song was for Jack, who's feeling blue about his girl. Sometimes, Jack, you've got to wonder if any girl can be worth all that heartache. You know what I mean?"

Sylvie had heard Jack call the previous night, too. He sounded young—still school-aged. Sylvie wondered why his parents let him stay up so late on weeknights.

"Here's another song," Georgia said, "'How Come You Don't Call Me' by Alicia Keys. This is dedicated to anyone else with love problems tonight."

As the next song began to play, Sylvie's thoughts drifted to her mother. She still missed her so much. They'd always been close. It was a cliché, maybe, but for her and her mother it had really been true. They'd been like best friends.

And even though her mother had struggled with diabetes most of her life, fifty had been too young for her to die. She'd always been so health conscious, so careful to manage her disease as well as she could.

Sylvie rolled over to her side and admired Reid's profile. He had small, even features, curly blond hair. In sleep he looked so much younger than his thirty-five years.

What would her mom have thought about him? About Sylvie having an affair with a married man?

The guilt that suddenly curdled in her stomach was her answer.

"What are you doing, Sylvie?"

She started at the unexpected sound of Reid's voice, so close. His eyes were open now, and he shifted to face her.

"I thought you were sleeping." She brushed a strand of hair off his forehead.

"I hate having to get up and leave you after we make love."

He pulled her in close so she could rest her head

on his chest. She inhaled the scent of him, of their lovemaking. Felt her nerves calm.

"I hate that, too."

A new song started playing on the radio, and they stayed cuddled together, listening. A few times Sylvie felt herself drifting off to sleep, but she always managed to rouse herself. She wanted to enjoy every moment in Reid's arms.

When the song ended, Reid eased his hold on her. "I have to go."

She knew better than to protest, planting just one sweet kiss on his cheek before rolling over to her side of the bed. In the faint golden glow from a lamp in the corner of the room, she watched as he gathered his clothes from the floor.

He went into her bathroom to shower. Reid always took a long time to clean himself up before going home to his wife. He even used a roller brush on his clothes to make sure he didn't miss even one strand of her red hair.

Once he came out of the bathroom, she wouldn't be able to kiss him. He didn't even like her to touch him.

Is this what you really want, Sylvie?

It was her mother's voice, but Sylvie refused to listen. She'd started this affair knowing the rules. Knowing that one day Reid would walk out her door and never return.

Only suddenly she was wondering if the story really had to end that way. Reid loved her. Maybe he would divorce his wife. Surely it was at least possible the two of them might have a future together....

"See you on Sunday?" Reid stood in the doorway. Other than his wet hair—which he would be able to explain away with the rain—he looked exactly the same as when he'd arrived hours earlier.

She nodded, hating herself for accepting so eagerly whatever crumbs of time he had to offer. How had this happened? When had this fun little adventure turned into something so very important to her?

Two hours into Georgia's program, Monty tapped on the window to the news bullpen. Georgia smiled and waved for him to come in. She'd just put on a song and had four minutes and thirty seconds before she needed to go on air again. She removed her headphones and finger-combed her hair back from her face.

"Got you hot chocolate." Monty handed her a tall paper cup with a plastic lid.

"Perfect." She removed the lid and poured the cocoa into her insulated KXPG mug. It would stay warm most of the night that way. "This is just what I need. Thanks, Monty."

"Hey, where are your flowers?"

"They were almost dead," she fibbed, "so I put them in the trash. Did you see that look Larry just gave me?"

Her producer had all but scowled at her through their shared window. The frosty reception he'd given her when she'd first started at KXPG hadn't thawed by one degree in the months they'd worked together. Georgia's efforts to be friendly had been spurned often enough that she'd stopped trying.

"Don't take him personally," Monty counseled. "He's just upset that you replaced Rachel Masterson."

Georgia knew the other woman had been on the late-night shift before her. "Are they friends?"

"More than friends, according to Larry."

"I see. No wonder he resents me."

"That's his problem."

She wished that were true. The success of her show depended on her and Larry working well together. She wished she could think of some way to appease him, short of stepping away from this job, which she would never do.

She'd worked hard for this opportunity and Mark Evans, the program director, had seen fit to give it to her. Ratings, so far, had been favorable so it seemed unlikely Mark would reverse his decision.

"I'm sure he'll come around eventually," Monty said. "I can't see anyone being able to stay mad at you for long."

"Thanks, Monty." Lucky for her not all the staff at KXPG disliked her. "Where did you work before you came here?"

"I used to be a pharmacist."

"Really? Why did you switch careers?" Surely the pay—and the hours—would be much better as a pharmacist.

"After almost thirty years, I needed a change. You get tired of talking to sick people all the time. Listening to them complain. Old ladies were the worst."

"They must have been lonely."

"That's the truth, but I didn't have time to spend half an hour counseling each of my customers." He shrugged. "I like working here, being around you young folk. Helps take my mind off Nancy."

"I'm glad." She wanted to ask him more about his career change, but Larry was waving at her to get ready to go on the air. Monty, used to interpreting the signals, too, quietly backed out of her room.

Georgia leaned up to her mike. "That was Chaka Khan, wondering 'Do you love me still?' Did you happen to notice the majestic piano playing in that piece? None other than Bruce Hornsby. And now I have a caller who wonders if his ex-girlfriend loves him anymore. Apparently they had a fight but he wants to make amends."

Seamlessly, Georgia queued in the prerecorded call.

THE MORNING CREW, ensconced in their much larger studio on the other side of the building, took over the airwaves from Georgia at 5:00 a.m. Georgia stood up from her desk and stretched out her arms, satisfied with the way the program had gone. She checked on Larry and saw him busy as usual, avoiding her gaze.

Should she extend the olive branch again? Remembering what Monty had told her about Rachel and Larry being an item, she decided to give it a shot.

She left her studio and rapped tentatively on his door. He glanced over his shoulder as she slipped into the room. In his thirties, Larry was a small man with a neat goatee and trendy, wire-rimmed glasses.

She attempted to sound upbeat and happy to see him. "Hey, Larry. How are you doing? That went pretty good, don't you think?"

"Not bad."

She'd had a record number of callers. Almost all had commented on how much they loved the new show.

She paused for a second to regroup, determined not to let his morose tone get her down. "Look, we may have started off on the wrong foot, but you're an excellent producer with a lot to offer my show. I'm hoping we can adjust to working together. If *Seattle after Midnight* becomes syndicated, as I hope it will, both our careers will profit."

"Not necessarily. This is your show. They can always hire another producer."

Was Larry throwing the gauntlet? "Is that what you want them to do?"

"No." But his eyes were full of venom as he pulled his glasses off, then carefully folded them into a leather holder. "I just happen to be one of the people who preferred Rachel's show. She had energy. Opinions. She wasn't afraid to make the program about more than broken hearts and lonely losers."

Broken hearts and lonely losers? Thanks a lot, Larry. But this wasn't the first time he'd compared her unfavorably to the woman who had covered the time slot before Georgia. At least now she understood why.

"My theory is that people have had enough of politics and current events by midnight. The late hours are the perfect time for reflection, and if that includes assessing your love life, your successes and failures, then that's okay."

"That's your opinion, obviously." Larry shrugged. "Is there anything else you need to talk about for tomorrow's show?"

Briefly they went over a few points of business. At least here, Larry was moderately cooperative. When they were done, Georgia decided against asking him to join her at the coffee shop, as she'd originally intended. Obviously he was determined to maintain the distance between them.

"I guess we're done." She turned to leave, but he stopped her with a question.

"What's with the flowers? Your birthday or something?"

Would he care if it was? "No, just a gift from a listener, I guess."

"They didn't come with a note?"

Why was he so curious? "Not a signed one."

"I see. A secret admirer." While Monty had been kindly teasing when he'd made the suggestion earlier, Larry seemed to be sneering at the idea. As if the possibility that she might have an admirer struck him as extremely unlikely.

Georgia thought of Pierce's reluctance to make even the slightest romantic overture. Well, maybe Larry had a point. In South Dakota she'd had no trouble attracting men. Perhaps her brand of sex appeal didn't translate to the Seattle market.

Thinking of South Dakota, though, led to a new theory about the flowers. Craig hadn't been very happy about their breakup. Could the roses be his way of trying to woo her back?

She wished it could be true. Flowers from Craig would be a problem she could easily handle. But the odds were slim. Craig had never been the sort for romantic gestures. And surely, if he'd gone to the expense of sending flowers, he would have included a signed card. What benefit would the gift be if she didn't know it came from him?

LARRY WAS long gone by the time Georgia grabbed her black case, then flicked out the lights in her studio. She wound her way down the two flights of stairs and stopped to say good-night to Monty. His shift didn't end until a full hour after hers.

"Sizemore didn't look too happy on his way out the door today," Monty commented.

"Maybe he thinks if he's miserable enough to me, I'll go back to South Dakota and his girlfriend will get her job back."

"I doubt if that would happen. Rachel's a great gal, but she's damn opinionated and she loves to talk. She didn't create the right mood for this time slot. Not like you. You're perfect for late-night radio."

"Thanks, Monty. You're great for my morale."

His smile was a little shy, but pleased. "Want me to walk you to your car tonight?"

Thinking of the latest delivery, Georgia decided to take him up on his offer. "That would be great."

He bounded out from behind the desk, pulling out his key ring as he moved.

"A pretty girl like you needs to be careful," he cautioned as he held the door open for her.

As she stepped out into the chill air she hoped she wouldn't find another rose in her car. She drew her trench coat tightly to her body and glanced out at the still-dark sky. It wouldn't be light for hours, at this time of year.

"At least it isn't raining."

"Give it five minutes," Monty predicted. He held out his hand for the keys she'd retrieved from her

purse, then stepped ahead to open her driver-
side door.

No rose. Thank goodness.

Georgia glanced across the parking lot, focusing
on the adjoining street where Pierce had been parked.
The street was bare this morning.

No big surprise. She'd had no reason to suppose
Pierce would come back. But at her feeling of vague
disappointment, she realized she'd nursed the hope.

Why was the man so blasted hard to forget?

"Thanks, Monty. See you tomorrow."

"You take care, Georgia."

Monty gave her a quick wave, then ran back to his
post. Georgia started the engine and began to drive.
As she traveled the familiar route home, she wondered what Pierce was doing right now. Was he still
on his surveillance job? Or home in bed like the ma-
jority of Seattle citizens?

Had he listened to her show tonight?

And why did she care so much?

She was such a fool.

At home she fell asleep shortly after she settled
into bed and didn't wake up until two o'clock in the
afternoon. First thing she checked her answering
machine. She had a message from her parents, who
must have called when she was at work, but nothing
from Pierce.

Again, no big surprise. What had she been
expecting?

Her parents wanted to confirm the arrival time and flight number of her trip home for Christmas. Because Christmas Eve fell on a Friday this year, and she had to work, she wouldn't be arriving until afternoon on Christmas Day. She called her mom and gave her all the details, then took out her Day-Timer and penciled in the engagements Mark Evans had told her about during their meeting the previous day.

In the radio business there were always lots of extra Christmas commitments. She'd be spending the next three Sundays wrapping presents at Bellevue Square, with proceeds going to the local food bank. And on this Saturday night she had a special emcee job at a holiday party for the kids at the Children's Hospital. Given her job and these worthwhile community events, she was glad she'd finished her shopping early.

A full week went by with no word from Pierce. The following Sunday, after her stint at Bellevue Square, Georgia invited Fred over for dinner.

"What happened to that cop who installed your security system a while ago?" Fred asked from his place at her table.

She spooned pot roast onto his plate. "Pierce Harding?" She tried to say the name as if she hadn't thought about the man constantly since she'd met him.

"Yeah. He seemed like a good guy, if a little rough around the edges."

"He isn't a cop, Fred. He's a private investigator."

Fred waved off the distinction. "Has he called?"

"No."

Fred made a noise of surprise.

Georgia didn't even try to pretend she didn't care. "I guess he isn't interested in me that way."

"I don't believe that for a moment, Georgie-girl. I saw the way that man looked at you."

"Well, I haven't heard from him since he installed the darn security system." She'd had several false alarms go off this week and was starting to think the system was more trouble than it was worth.

"Did he send you a bill for his work?"

"Well…no."

"He's going to call." Fred took the pitcher of gravy and poured it generously over his plate.

Georgia knew better than to argue. Fred, dear soul, thought she was irresistible. But Pierce wasn't going to contact her. If she wanted to see him again, it would have to be on her own initiative.

But there was only one possible reason for her to do that and since the delivery of the three roses at work the previous week, she'd had no further contact from her secret admirer. She'd even decided against calling the police since the man seemed to have tired of his little game.

Whoever her admirer had been, he'd obviously lost interest. And she was glad. She'd had no calls from Jack this week, either, which fueled her belief that he'd been the one sending the flowers.

"I could see it in his eyes." Fred would not let the subject drop. "When a man gets that spellbound glaze, he's lost. No sense even trying to fight it."

Spellbound glaze? Pierce Harding? Poor old Fred must be developing cataracts.

Still, after dinner, when Fred had returned to his side of the duplex, Georgia pondered his words. Was Fred just an old fogy who couldn't tell Pierce had put in that security system out of a sense of obligation and responsibility?

Or were his instincts right?

She, too, had been so sure she'd seen signs of attraction when Pierce looked at her. Had she misread the signals? Was she just too unsophisticated for him?

Or did the problem lie elsewhere? Like with his dead wife, for instance?

Georgia told herself to just forget about him. But she couldn't and it was darn frustrating. Something—maybe the aura of mystery surrounding him—kept calling to her. If she knew more about him, maybe she could understand why he held himself at such distance from people. From her.

Her curiosity nagged and nagged until finally she decided she could at least find out the details of his wife's car accident. The story had probably been covered in the local paper.

Monday morning, almost two weeks from the day

she'd met Pierce, she searched the public library microfiche records of the *Seattle Times*. Within half an hour she found what she was looking for.

"Police Officer's Wife in Coma after Collision." That was the first story, and Georgia's heart raced with empathetic anxiety as she read the details and imagined how devastating this must have been for Pierce.

Four days later, another article made headlines on the City Page. "Police Officer's Wife Dies After Four-Day Coma." Farther down the page she read: "Officer Pierce Harding never left his wife's side."

Her name had been Cassandra. There was a photo of Pierce and his bride together at some police function. Georgia studied the image carefully but it was a full-body shot and she couldn't see either of their faces very clearly.

As for the car accident itself, the facts seemed puzzling. Apparently Cassandra had been driving on the wrong side of Aurora Avenue—old Highway 99—when her vehicle had been struck by an oncoming truck. The driver of the truck had survived. There were no charges laid.

Georgia read both articles carefully, but no reason was given for why Cassandra was driving on the wrong side of the road. According to witnesses, she'd been in the left-hand lane for several seconds— long enough to have corrected an accidental wrenching of the wheel.

How awful. How strange. Why had she made such a grievous mistake? Georgia had traveled that route a few times herself and while no physical barrier divided north- and southbound lanes on that stretch of highway, the centerline was well marked. According to the article, the weather and road conditions were not to blame.

Perhaps Cassandra had suffered a stroke or a heart attack?

Georgia could find no further clues in the newspaper.

CHAPTER SIX

AFTER HER Monday night show, Georgia felt more tired than usual. She drove home through the rain feeling as if her mind was going numb from the endless parade of gray, damp days. Locals told her that usually they had at least a brief glimpse of the sun in the afternoons, but this last week had been particularly gloomy. As Georgia nosed her car into the driveway beside her house, she recalled the way bright sunshine reflecting off the fields of snow back home had sometimes given her a headache.

That was one headache she wouldn't mind having today.

Trudging up the walk, she considered not checking on Fred, but her conscience wouldn't let her get away with that. With more effort than usual, she crossed the hedge and tested his door.

Unlocked again. Wearily, she pulled out her keys and turned the dead bolt.

Then she headed to her own home, slipping in the front door and dumping off her bag and wet coat.

She was in the kitchen, when she realized something was wrong.

She'd forgotten to enter her security code on the remote control by the front door, yet the alarm hadn't gone off. Powered by adrenaline now, she hurried to the panel by the back door and saw that the system wasn't activated.

How was that possible? She was sure she'd set it on her way to work the previous evening.

A cold shiver crept up her spine. She grabbed the phone and with her fingers poised to dial 911, she checked the windows and back door on the main floor. All were locked and undamaged. None of her electronic equipment was missing. Her extensive, and irreplaceable, CD collection seemed to be intact.

She climbed the stairs next. The bathroom looked fine, as did her office.

She stopped at the threshold to her bedroom and was about to breathe a final sigh of relief, when she saw the rose. It had been placed in a vase and left on her nightstand. One, single, bloodred rose, its perfume so fragrant she could smell it from the bedroom doorway.

He'd been in here. In her bedroom. How was that possible? She was *certain* she'd set the alarm on her way out. Yet somehow he'd deactivated it. The latch on the back door had been fastened and the front door had been locked, which meant he definitely had a key.

Oh, God, no. She didn't want to believe any of this, but the perfect rose at the side of her bed mocked her. *I was here.* She wanted to hurl the vase out the window. Instead, leaning against the door frame of her bedroom, fingers shaking, she dialed the police.

"I need to report a break-in to my home on Belmont Avenue."

She answered questions, provided her name, address and telephone number. Since nothing had been stolen and there seemed to be no damage, she was told an officer would come out to get her signed report the next day.

She stood in the center of her bedroom and knew that wasn't enough. Her home had been invaded. Finally, she gave in to the craving to call Pierce.

She didn't have the energy to try his office number and risk going through his receptionist, whom she had ended up speaking to for fifteen minutes the first time she'd called. So she called his cell phone. He picked up after two rings.

"Harding."

"Pierce? This is Georgia. I just found another rose. In my bedroom." Her teeth were chattering. Must be shock. She went to the closet and wrapped herself in a thick wool sweater.

"Your *bedroom?* How'd he get inside?"

Pierce sounded livid, as if this were somehow her fault.

"I don't know! I set the alarm and locked the front door before I left last night to do my show. I just got home about ten minutes ago, and the alarm wasn't on. As far as I can tell, nothing has been stolen or damaged. But there's a rose in a vase on my bedside table."

Pierce cursed. "Did you phone the cops?"

"They're sending someone out tomorrow."

"Okay. Let me see…"

She heard something creaking. Bed springs?

"Give me fifteen minutes," he finally said. "I'll be there as soon as I can."

Thank God. She was sorry she'd probably gotten him out of bed, but this whole thing was getting out of hand. Maybe Pierce could help her figure out what to do.

She went downstairs and waited by the front window until she saw his car pull up. She opened the door for him before he had a chance to knock.

"Am I glad to see you." And she was. She'd never seen a more reassuring sight in her life.

Pierce strode into the hall, his gaze already sweeping the surroundings. "Nothing on the main floor was touched?"

"No."

He picked up the remote control for the security system and made sure it was working. Then he turned to her. "He left the rose upstairs?"

"Yes. In my bedroom."

Pierce took the stairs two at a time and she followed. By the time she caught up he was already by the vase.

"Have you read the note?"

She'd been so stunned, she'd forgotten to check for one. But yes, she could see the piece of paper now, wrapped around the stem as before.

"Sit down," Pierce instructed.

She did, on the side of the bed. Pierce settled next to her, then handed her the note. They read it together, Pierce looking over her shoulder, his leg and his arm touching hers.

Only six more to go. Georgia, I love you.

"Oh, God." Before today, she'd never truly felt worried. But now she was terrified. "He knows where I live, where I work, the car I drive. He knows everything about me."

"While we know nothing about him." Pierce took the note from her. "It says only six more to go. But this is just the third rose."

"Actually, he sent me three others." She told him about the delivery to the radio station.

"You're kidding. God, why didn't you call me?"

"I thought about it. But then more than a week passed with nothing happening. I hoped this was finally over…."

Pierce moved from the bed to the window, scanning the neighborhood, as if he hoped to find the man responsible so easily. He swiveled to face her. "When you left your home for work, you're sure you didn't forget to set the alarm?"

"I remember locking the door. The system was on." She was positive about this. "When I arrived home and saw that the alarm had been deactivated, I immediately knew someone had been here."

"You should have gone to Fred's at that point. Georgia, he might still have been in your house."

She decided not to mention that she'd had the phone in her hands ready to call emergency. He would only point out—correctly—that if the man had jumped her, or had a gun, she never would have had a chance to make that call.

Had a gun.

Georgia started to tremble. This couldn't be happening. How could an innocent flower and note left on her car have led to something this scary?

"If all he wanted was to leave me another flower and a note, why did he go to the trouble of breaking into my house? He could have left them on the porch like he did before."

She hadn't seen Pierce this angry before. This intense.

"It's an act of aggressive intimacy. He's been in your personal living space now. He's seen the table where you eat your meals. The bed where you sleep."

Georgia jumped off the mattress, suddenly sure that he had touched the bed. Perhaps even lain down on it. She'd thought the covers looked a little messy….

She yanked the duvet off the bed. "I have to wash this. I can't stand to think of him here."

Pierce helped her unfasten the snaps and pull the feather comforter out from its cover.

"Oh, I hate this. I hate it!" She pulled off the pillowcases and then the sheets. "Why is he doing this? What does he want from me?"

"He's a disturbed man who heard you on the radio and became fixated with you. For a while his fantasies probably kept him satisfied. Now, he's decided he needs more."

She balled the sheets in her arms. "That doesn't sound like Jack. He called my show again last night and he sounded so sweet and lonely. Not the sort of person to do something like this."

Pierce shrugged. "You can't be sure, Georgia."

She stared at the sheets in her hands. They felt soiled to her. She would have to use bleach to get them clean. "The washing machine is in the basement," she told Pierce. "I'll just be a minute."

THOUGH TEMPTED to linger in Georgia's bedroom for a few moments longer—there were photos on the dresser he'd like to have studied, plus he was curious about the stack of books next to her bed—Pierce followed Georgia down the stairs, then waited in the kitchen.

Tea was good for someone who'd just had a shock, wasn't it? He filled the kettle and plugged it in. Found a tea bag and put it into a KXPG mug.

While he waited for the water to boil, he checked the windows and back door for himself. As Georgia had said, there were no signs that anyone had tampered with these entry points.

Yet someone had been in here. He had only to recall Georgia's pale, shocked face to know how badly she'd been frightened. He thought of his description of the person who had done this:

He's a disturbed man who heard you on the radio and became fixated with you.

Pierce wondered if Georgia realized that that description applied to him as well as it did to the man who'd broken into this house.

Hadn't he listened to Georgia's program so much that he'd become obsessed with her, too? In fact, his obsession had taken such control over him that he'd actually driven by her radio station on the off chance that he would see her.

He wasn't much better than the stalker. He'd taken advantage of an innocent young woman's loneliness and used it to his own advantage. He'd needed every ounce of his self-control this past week to keep from phoning her. A few times he'd even driven by her house in the early morning hours to make sure she'd arrived home safely after work.

He'd hoped that a little distance would cool his feelings for her, but his enforced absence had had the exact opposite effect.

Now that he was with her again, he wanted her

more than before…and that was saying a lot. He could no longer pretend he had the self-control to stay away.

How could he protect her from this stalker, when he might cause her the most harm of all?

Leave, he told himself. He could go now while she was in the basement. Tomorrow he'd phone her with a reference for another private investigator. Oh, she'd be a little hurt, but in the long run she'd be better off.

It was a good plan, but Pierce couldn't make himself take his own advice.

Who could I find who would watch out for her the way I can? And how could he live with the guilt if he stepped aside and something happened to her?

Hearing her footsteps on the stairs, he turned to the kettle, now boiling steadily.

"Well, that's done." She entered the kitchen with empty hands.

"I'm making some tea. Let's sit down for a minute. We need to have a discussion."

He didn't tell her that he was afraid he might be more dangerous to her than the stalker. He didn't warn her to keep her distance, that he was a bad risk romantically speaking and in most other ways, too. Instead he concentrated on sounding cool and professional.

"Let's take a look at all the notes he's left you so far." He reached into his jacket pocket. "I brought the first two with me. I'm assuming there was a note with the third delivery, too?"

"Yes. It's in my bag." Georgia went to the hall to retrieve it.

"Okay," Pierce laid them out on the table in the order they'd been received. "The first note says 'A dozen roses, then you'll be mine….'"

Georgia put a hand to her throat. "He's already sent me half a dozen." She looked at him wide-eyed.

"Right. That's what he said in the fourth note. The second note lets you know he's been watching you, and the third note says, 'Counting the days.'" Pierce shook his head. "The guy obviously has a plan. I wish the hell I knew what it was."

"If his plan is to scare me to death, it's working."

Pierce felt a strong urge to take her into his arms and offer comfort. Knowing he didn't dare do that, he concentrated again on being analytical. "Consider the overall pattern here. The first rose was left on the exterior of your car. The next one was on your front porch."

Georgia nodded, "Then three were delivered to my office."

"Anyone familiar with your show would know where you work. All he'd have to do is follow you home one day to discover your residential address."

"That's right." One of her small hands was wrapped around the mug he'd given her. The other was splayed on the kitchen table and he couldn't help but notice how fragile her bones appeared, how pale her skin.

Her utter vulnerability scared the crap out of him.

Focus, he reminded himself. "But getting access to the interior of your home—that's another thing entirely. You said the front door was locked and the alarm was set. That means he had a key and your security code."

"Yes, but how on earth did he get them?"

"How many keys do you have?"

"Only two. One is on my key chain. I usually keep that in my bag."

"And the other?"

"Fred and I exchanged keys shortly after I moved in."

"Fred." He thought about that for a moment. "And the combination code for your alarm?"

"I input it into my Palm Pilot, in case I forgot it. The Palm Pilot was also in my bag. But no one could access the information recorded there without my password."

"So no one else knows your security code?"

"Except Fred. I had to give him the code in case it goes off when I'm at work. Or in the event I have some sort of emergency like a leaking water pipe and he needs access to my place."

Pierce raised his eyebrows. "Fred, again. I guess we've found our weakest link."

"How can you say that? You've met him—do you really think he would break into my apartment?" Her eyes widened. "You're not suggesting he's the one who's been giving me the roses?"

"It's not impossible, but not likely, either. Fred himself provided the clue to all this. Remember when he said he'd noticed a man in a strange car hanging around the neighborhood?"

"Yes. But how could a stranger get my key? My private security code?"

"A person wouldn't have to observe you for long to realize the tight bond between you and Fred. I'm guessing that our stalker figured Fred would have your spare key and the code for your alarm. Neighbors tend to watch out for one another, after all, and you're new to town, without friends or family nearby."

The stalker would know all this, because Georgia did talk about herself on her program. She was sure she'd mentioned missing her family and close friends. Her willingness to share her own life with her listeners was part of what made them able to relate to her.

"Are you saying the stalker found my key and code at Fred's?"

"His place is a lot easier to break into than yours. Didn't you say that he sometimes forgets to lock his own door?"

"That's true," she admitted. "Poor Fred. He'll never forgive himself if we find out that's what really happened."

"But we need to find out. If the stalker has your key, you'll have to change the locks. You need to input a different security code, too."

"Right." She stood with a sigh and went to the control panel. Following the steps he'd outlined for her on the day he installed the system, she changed the code to a different four numeral pattern.

"Now let's go talk to Fred."

"We can't. He'll be sleeping now then going to the community center. He plays shuffleboard on Tuesday mornings."

"Okay, we'll have to do that later."

Pierce noticed her stifle a yawn. "You must be tired. You usually sleep after your show, don't you?"

"I don't think I can go back into my bedroom yet," she confessed.

"Why don't you nap on the couch? I have some calls I need to make and paperwork to take care of. I can work in your kitchen for a few hours—that way you'll know you're safe."

He could tell she wanted to accept his offer, but she said, "That's okay. I've taken enough of your time today."

He thought of the extra assignments he'd already given Will and Jake because of her. The longer hours he himself had put in these past couple of weeks. "It's no trouble. December's one of our slower months," he lied. "Hang tight while I get my stuff from the car."

GEORGIA SLEPT surprisingly well for about four hours. It was eleven when she awoke. She could hear

Pierce talking on the phone in her kitchen, though she couldn't make out what he was saying.

She ran upstairs to wash and change into fresh clothes before seeking him out.

Though he had his back to her, sitting at the table facing her yard, he seemed to sense her presence right away.

"Sleep okay?"

"Fantastic. Thanks so much for staying." No way could she have relaxed, otherwise.

"No problem. I guess I should be leaving...."

He'd been so kind rushing to her aid like this. Yet he acted like it was nothing. Did anyone ever offer to help him with his problems, she wondered?

"I went to the library on Saturday and looked up the details of your wife's car accident. Pierce, I'm so sorry."

She'd caught him off guard with this. "I hope you don't think I was prying by checking the newspapers."

He turned his head slightly away from her, something she'd noticed him do before when the conversation turned personal.

"I don't make a secret of what happened to Cass."

No, but she figured he didn't talk about it much, either. Which was a shame, because it was her guess that a little talking would do this guy a world of good. But not here. Maybe she'd have more luck on neutral territory.

"Would you like to go out for lunch?" she asked, expecting him to turn her down.

But he surprised her. "There's a deli by my office. How does that sound?"

"Great."

CHAPTER SEVEN

THE DELI WAS brightly lit and busy, but Georgia and Pierce managed to find a booth by a window. They doctored their sandwiches from a selection of mustards on the table, and Georgia added as much cream to her coffee as she had room for.

For a few moments they ate in silence. Pierce's dark eyes were heavy with fatigue. He hadn't shaved that morning and the shadow on his lower jaw made him look slightly menacing.

Across the street, Christmas lights on a mom-and-pop hardware store were blurry through the afternoon rain. The city was endlessly gray and wet. When her mother had called yesterday, she'd reported a huge dump of snow. At least Georgia could look forward to a white Christmas in South Dakota.

Pierce seemed to guess the direction of her thoughts. "Are you heading home for the holidays?"

"I am. I booked my flights shortly after I moved here. Though I'll only have two nights off from work, it'll be worth the money and time spent traveling. What about you? What do you do for Christmas?"

"I've never celebrated the holiday."

"Religious reasons?"

"No. I just don't like Christmas."

What he said was so absurd she couldn't help but smile. "Come on. What about when you were a kid?"

"Especially when I was kid."

Her smile faded. She'd had earlier hints that his childhood had been hard. But not to have celebrated Christmas… "What about when you were married? Don't tell me you didn't put up a Christmas tree in your house? Surely you and Cassandra exchanged presents?"

"Cass did the tree thing and the turkey dinner. But I was a real Scrooge. I used to spoil her on her birthday to make up for it."

"That's not the same," she chided gently.

Pierce didn't answer. His gaze drifted to the slightly garish light display at the hardware store, and Georgia wondered if not celebrating Christmas with his wife was a regret of his.

"What happened with that job you were working on? The one with the husband out of town on business?" Pierce hadn't used names when he'd discussed it before. Confidentiality reasons, obviously.

Pierce shrugged. "The day her husband was scheduled to return to town, the wife left the hotel and drove to the airport to pick him up. They went home."

"Did you ever figure out what she was doing in the hotel?"

"Writing. She'd packed a laptop computer and a laser printer in her suitcase."

"Seriously?"

"Apparently for the past year or so she's been booking herself into hotel rooms for the odd day or weekend in order to work on a novel."

Well, that was a twist. "How did you find this out?"

"I asked her."

"What?" Georgia laughed. "Isn't that against the rules or something?"

"I made up a story about how I was staying at the hotel, too, and had noticed she was putting in long hours. I did my best to be charming, if you can imagine such a thing."

Oh, she could imagine. Pierce smiling as the woman opened the door. *I couldn't help being curious,* he would have said.

"She had no trouble telling me, a perfect stranger, what she was up to. But apparently she was too self-conscious to confide in her husband."

Georgia could understand that. "Because her husband's opinion would be so important to her."

"I guess."

"But if he was out of town, she would have had the house to herself. Why did she book into a hotel?"

"Apparently there were too many distractions at home."

"What did her husband say when he found out what she was doing?"

"He was pretty damned relieved she wasn't having an affair."

Georgia laughed, then the momentary distraction of Pierce's case faded, and she began to think about his wife again. According to the paper, they'd been married three years.

"How did you and Cassandra meet?"

Pierce looked annoyed at the question, but he answered. "She was a social worker. I met her at work. I'd been called to the scene of a domestic dispute. The father was a waster, the mother a drunk with bad taste in boyfriends. Cass became involved on behalf of the two small kids."

Pierce supplied few details, but from the expression on his face, Georgia could tell that something about this particular case had hit him hard.

"Did the kids end up okay?"

"They were put into foster homes." He shrugged. "Cass did the best she could for them. But eventually they were returned to the mother. One of them ended up being beaten really badly by the boyfriend. Cass was devastated. She always thought she could save the world if she only had enough time and resources."

"It sounds like she was a good person."

"It wasn't right for her to die. Not so young." Pierce gazed out the window.

"The accident happened on Christmas Eve," Georgia recalled. Given Pierce's distaste for the holiday, that seemed painfully ironic.

"She'd just decorated our tree the night before. We'd had the usual fight over me not helping."

"Where were you when it happened?"

"I was on duty that afternoon." He turned away from the window, but his eyes had a faraway look, as if he were not just remembering the past, but reliving it.

"How did you hear about the accident?"

"The report of a head-on collision on Aurora Avenue came over the radio, as usual. I heard a woman had been seriously injured, but I never guessed... I was busy with my own work, on the lookout for some teenaged vandals who'd just trashed a bunch of Christmas lights on an old lady's house. Not that I couldn't sympathize with the vandals in that case."

"What about your wife, Pierce? When did you find out she was the one...?"

"The cops on the scene IDed her from her driver's license. My name was listed on her insurance card." Pierce focused on his hands, as he relayed the last of his story. "I was asked to report in at the station. My partner met me at the door. He took me into one of the meeting rooms. Our sergeant was waiting. Together they told me what had happened."

What a miserable conversation that must have been. Georgia wanted to reach out to Pierce, just touch his hand in sympathy. But he was holding his body stiff and aloof from her.

"They didn't want me anywhere near the collision scene, but I couldn't stop myself. Their description of the accident didn't make sense. Cass was an excellent driver. She'd never had so much as a fender bender before."

Of course, he would go to the scene. Georgia knew him well enough to understand that. "Was Cassandra still there?"

"No. The ambulance had left by the time I arrived. The traffic team was in the midst of the collision investigation. They showed me exactly what happened."

"Oh, Pierce."

"I guess you read about it in the newspaper articles, huh? She was driving on the wrong side of the road for at least five seconds." He shook his head, as if he still couldn't believe it. "Sounds so quick, five seconds, but it isn't. Five seconds on the wrong side of a busy city freeway is…a death sentence."

Georgia had already gone through the mental exercise of counting out the time in her head and she agreed with him. While she could imagine several scenarios that might cause a driver to accidentally cross the yellow line for a second or two, five seconds was too long.

Something had happened.

"Several oncoming cars managed to avoid her by

swerving wildly. Even when they honked their horns, she still didn't get over into the correct lane."

"The article said driving conditions weren't to blame."

"That's right. For once it wasn't raining and it wasn't yet dark, so visibility shouldn't have been a problem."

"Could there have been a medical explanation? Maybe a stroke or a seizure of some sort?"

"She had no preexisting condition, but that's what I thought, at first. Or maybe I should say I hoped—" Pierce's twisted smile revealed his predicament. "I needed to find an explanation, I was desperate to find an explanation."

"And did you ever?"

He shook his head. "The investigation came up with nothing. The car was fine, there'd been no mechanical failure. And the autopsy didn't reveal anything, either. I spoke to Cass's doctor. And to her friends and her parents. No one could offer any excuse for what happened."

Pierce had given up on his sandwich a while ago. Now he sipped at his coffee and gazed blankly out the window.

Georgia sought another rational explanation. "Was she drinking coffee? Trying to put on her lipstick?"

"No cup was found in the car. No food of any kind. She didn't have her cell phone with her so she couldn't have been trying to answer it or to place a call."

His pain was obvious as he rehashed points he must have gone over in his own mind countless times.

"She could have been distracted by a hundred different things," Georgia reasoned. "Maybe she was trying to change the CD or to adjust her seat. Maybe she heard something upsetting on the radio...."

"Everything you say is possible," Pierce admitted.

She studied his expression, her own heart aching.

Pain mingled with something else, something she'd sensed in him before. Regret? Guilt? She recalled his comment about the argument the night before the accident. "Did you and Cass happen to fight about something more serious than Christmas decorations?"

Pierce didn't say anything for a while. Finally he shifted in his seat and nodded. "Cass wanted to start a family even though I'd told her when we decided to get married that I didn't want kids."

"But she married you anyway?"

"I guess she thought I'd change my mind. There were lots of things Cass wanted me to change."

"Like...?" Georgia prodded.

"She wanted me to quit the police force."

Which he'd done after his wife's death. Had he made the decision as a tribute to Cassandra?

"Sometimes I think Cass thought of me as another one of her clients. A long-term project," he added ironically. "Maybe she hoped once she'd 'cured' me, I'd magically turn into a perfect husband and father."

"Cured you of what, Pierce?"

For the first time in their conversation, he looked at her intently. One side of his mouth turned up with amusement. "You ask all the tough questions, Georgia."

"While you avoid all the tough answers."

He raised his eyebrows, refusing to accept the bait.

"So what about the day of the accident?" Georgia asked. "Where was Cassandra going?"

"She was on her way to serve meals at a homeless shelter."

Of course. This Cassandra sounded like a paragon. Had she really married Pierce planning to change him? But why did Pierce need changing? Was it because of something from his past, his childhood in New York City?

"She should never have married me."

"Pierce, couples fight all the time. That argument doesn't make the accident your fault."

"I'm not talking just about the accident."

Had their marriage been very unhappy? Pierce had already intimated that they'd had their disagreements. Georgia opened her mouth to ask, but Pierce cut her off.

"Let's get out of here. Want to go for a drive?"

GEORGIA AND Pierce left their meals uneaten and went outside into the rain. Georgia slipped on the hood of her black slicker. Pierce didn't seem to notice the wetness soaking through his thick hair and washing the light stubble on his cheeks.

This was the first time he'd invited Georgia anywhere. Was it a sign that she was finally breaking through to him? Pierce unlocked the passenger side of his Nissan for her, then loped around the front of the car to the driver's door.

Inside the car, Georgia removed her slicker and finger-combed water droplets from her hair. Through the wet windshield the city looked vague and out of focus until Pierce started the car and turned on the wipers sending the excess water sluicing along the sides of the glass.

Pierce pulled into the midday traffic, merging onto Highway 5 headed south. Instead of turning off into the Capitol Hill area where Georgia lived, he exited west on Mercer Street, then headed north on Aurora Avenue.

Georgia sat, shocked and silent, as she realized he was tracing his wife's route on the day she had died. Neither one said a word as Pierce slowly positioned the car into the far left-hand lane.

Traffic was gearing up for the late-afternoon rush hour and Georgia, who still wasn't used to the volume of vehicles in a bigger metropolis, felt hemmed in by the sheer number of cars on all sides of them. She shuddered every time Pierce passed a semi or large bus.

"This is the spot where Cass started driving on the wrong side of the road." Pierce spoke without emotion, his profile grim, both hands clenched round the steering wheel.

In her head, Georgia began counting the seconds. *One-one-hundred; two-one-hundred; three-one-hundred...* As she marked the passage of time, she noted the clear delineation between north- and southbound lanes. She could see why Pierce found it impossible to believe his wife had simply made a driving error.

Just as she reached *five-one-hundred* in her counting, Pierce said, gruffly, "Here. This is where she had the crash."

Georgia swallowed a sudden shot of fear and tried not to imagine a car meeting a big semitruck head on.

"It couldn't have been an accident," Pierce said with frightening calm. "It isn't possible for a driver to make a mistake like that."

"Are you saying she did it on purpose?" That his wife had wanted to die?

Pierce didn't reply.

"Cassandra could have had a seizure the medics didn't pick up on. Maybe something happened on the side of the road to distract her."

"Yeah, like a spaceship trying to land from Mars?"

She wanted to scream with frustration at how stubborn he was. Then suddenly, in one flash of intuition, she understood perfectly what was going on.

She waited until his tension had cleared a little. They were headed back the way they'd come. She looked at his grim profile, so utterly masculine and strong.

"I don't think your wife's accident is the real mystery here."

His quick glance was uncomprehending.

"You want to know what puzzles me, Pierce? Why are you so desperate to find a way to blame yourself for her death? That's the real question you need to answer."

PIERCE DROVE back to his building, not planning what he would do when he got there. The drive had been a mistake. Showing Georgia where Cass had died, a serious error in judgment.

After he parked the Nissan in the underground garage he turned to Georgia. He should have taken her home.

So why hadn't he?

She returned his gaze earnestly, her emotions on clear display. Concern, compassion, warmth…and attraction.

Only a heel would take advantage of that last with a woman like her. Of course, he'd done it before with Cass. They'd started their relationship by going out for coffee to discuss the children they were trying to help.

Coffee had led to a lunch date. Lunch to dinner

and dinner to bed. Being with Cass had been so peaceful compared to his other relationships. Except for her annoying habit of analyzing everything he said or did.

Still, on balance he'd been happy with her, although he never would have opted for marriage if it hadn't been so important to her.

Just as it would undoubtedly be important to Georgia when she fell in love.

"Want to come in for a drink?" he invited.

"Okay," she said, as he'd guessed she would.

He led her to his studio apartment across the hall from his office, trying to tell himself that there was nothing wrong with what he was doing. He wasn't going to try to seduce Georgia.

So what do you want then, his inner voice mocked him. *Just to be friends?*

Noticing the sway of Georgia's hips as she walked into his place ahead of him, he knew that wasn't possible. He didn't have an answer for why he'd invited Georgia into his home. He just wanted to be with her.

After flicking on the gas fireplace, he poured them both a glass of wine. After that tense episode on the freeway, she seemed glad for the drink, as was he.

He switched on another bank of lights, bringing a bright halogen glow to showcase his framed collection of black-and-white cityscapes. The extra light also added a needed clarity to the setting.

They sat in the two swivel chairs near the fire. He watched Georgia take in the stark details of his colorless apartment. For the first time he wondered why he'd created such a contrast to the home his wife had made for them. Cass had worked hard to bring warmth and creature comforts to his life. But he'd never really felt at home there.

Where he'd grown up, families didn't eat meals together. They didn't share their dreams with each other, either, because if you were foolish enough to have a dream, you damn well kept it to yourself.

Cass could never get that. Could never accept that he wasn't the kind of man to build a family and a real home with.

"What's this?" Georgia rose from the chair and went to the sofa on the other side of a glass coffee table. She picked up one of Cass's cross-stitched pillows, the only one he'd kept.

"What beautiful work." She examined the garden scene closely and ran a hand lightly over the wool pattern.

"Cass made that. She transferred the pattern from a photograph I took." They'd been in England, on their honeymoon. A happy time, probably the happiest of his life. Maybe that was why he hadn't been able to part with that particular cushion.

Georgia set the cushion gently back where she'd found it. "Do you have a picture of her?"

He hesitated, then went to the kitchen and removed a photo from the fridge. The picture had been shot on the beach. Cass was lying on a towel, looking up at the camera and laughing. To him her tanned skin, wide smile and dancing eyes only affirmed her youth and good health, and added to the obscenity of her death. "This was taken the summer before she died."

"She was beautiful. And Pierce, she looks happy."

Yes, there'd been good times, he knew that. But he also knew there'd been occasions when he'd deeply disappointed her. In that last year, she'd often accused him of being cold and distant. Though he'd longed for the home and warmth Cass offered, something inside him was always pulling back.

"Did Cassandra have family in Seattle?"

"Her parents live in Spokane."

He watched Georgia settle on the swivel chair again and wondered what she was doing here. By all rights, she ought to be running as far away from him as possible.

"I don't get you, Georgia. Why would you want to hang around with a guy who has as many battle scars as I do?"

Her gaze flicked over the length of his body, then back to his face. "I like you, Pierce. I can't explain it. I can't fight it. I just like you."

Nothing she might have said to him could have affected him as powerfully as those simple words. *I like you.* She could have professed to be attracted to him, admitted that she wanted to sleep with him. He would have understood because he knew from experience that there were women who reacted to him that way.

But when she said she *liked* him, well, that felt directed to him as a person. His mind, his heart, hell maybe even his soul, if he had one.

His instinct was to counter with the argument that she didn't even know him. But he didn't believe that was true. He felt as if she did know him. Which made her statement all the more remarkable.

He had the urge to say, *I like you, too,* but surely that was redundant. How could anyone not like Georgia? While Cass had been a kind, good-intentioned person, there was something about Georgia that transcended all that.

She didn't judge, he realized. *She just listened.*

"I'm sick of all this focus about me and my life. Tell me some more about South Dakota. About what it was like to grow up on a farm."

"Pierce, you'll be bored."

"I doubt that." What she might think dull, he would find remarkable. Remarkable because it would be so very different from the way he'd been raised.

"Don't blame me if you fall asleep. Our dairy farm has been in our family for three generations. I have an older brother, Eric, and my mom and dad will have been married forty-one years this October…."

GEORGIA'S STORY didn't put Pierce to sleep. Her voice enchanted him, just as her radio program always did. He found himself itching to move closer to her, to touch her hand as she talked. She made it all seem so real, her childhood years on that farm in South Dakota. He could smell the turkey roasting on Christmas day, see the wildflowers blooming in the pasture in the spring, imagine the sound of her mother's voice calling her to breakfast every morning.

What he could not understand was how a woman with Georgia's past could talk about sadness and loneliness the way she did every night on her program. On the radio she sounded intimately acquainted with pain, sorrow, heartbreak and hopelessness.

At the end of an anecdote about her school years, she stopped reminiscing suddenly. "You'd let me talk all day, wouldn't you?"

"Absolutely."

"But you've got to be so *bored*."

"No. Just curious. On the radio you sound like you've seen it all. But your life has been so…happy. So uncomplicated."

"I know. By rights I should be chirping out weather reports on a morning wake-up program. But my grandmother always said I was born a wise old soul. And I am more of a night owl than a morning person."

Finally, one thing they had in common. But Pierce

knew he shouldn't be looking for things he had in common with this woman. He glanced at his watch and couldn't believe it was past dinnertime.

"Are you hungry?"

She patted her slender stomach. "Starving. We barely touched our sandwiches. Want to order pizza in or go out?"

She made the idea of their sharing this next meal, too, sound so casual, so easy. Against his smarter instincts, he picked up the phone and requested two medium pizzas—one vegetarian, one Meat Lover's. Before he rang off, Georgia said, "I hope you're not counting on me eating the vegetarian one."

"Make that one large Meat Lover's," he revised. After hanging up the phone, he went to the kitchen. "Another glass of wine? Or would you prefer a beer?"

"I'm easy."

That she was, he reflected as he poured from the open bottle of burgundy on the counter. In that respect she differed from Cass who had always had exacting ideas about everything from what she wanted to eat, to how the furniture should be placed, to how he ought to cut his hair.

"Can I put on some music?"

He heard her flipping through the CDs he had sorted alphabetically in the stereo cabinetry.

"Go ahead." He was curious about what she would choose, but he didn't recognize the music when it started. Maybe it was something of Cass's. Light jazz, a little romantic, but not overly so.

The pizza arrived and they ate on the floor, Georgia cross-legged again. She sat that way a lot, he'd noticed. Her casual style was part of what made him so comfortable around her.

"God, this is good pizza." She closed her eyes and swayed her head a little in time with the music.

He wondered if the pizza could really be that tasty. The more he watched her, though, the less he cared.

"Georgia." He wasn't hungry at all. Not for pizza, at least. She opened her eyes and looked at him. He couldn't stop himself from putting a hand behind her head.

"I shouldn't kiss you," he said.

"Why not?"

He didn't know how to begin to answer that question. Her past lay like a blameless white sheet behind her. His was checkered with alcoholic parents, juvenile acts of delinquency, and a first marriage that had ended in tragedy.

"I'm trying to do the right thing. You don't want to get involved with someone like me."

"You're right. I don't want someone like you. I want you."

The words made him almost crazy with need. God she was so direct, so open. She could be hurt so very easily….

She set down the glass of wine she'd been about to drink from and reached for his face. He felt her soft fingers brush against his cheek and run along the edge of his jaw.

"Georgia. *No.*"

"Not no." She leaned forward. *"Yes."*

CHAPTER EIGHT

DURING THE COURSE of her radio career, Georgia had heard all sorts of hard-luck stories from people who'd claimed they couldn't help falling in love with the wrong person. She was always sympathetic to these callers, but deep inside she couldn't help but wonder why they made such foolish choices.

Now, having met Pierce, she finally understood how pure longing could overpower the logical side of the brain. She didn't care about anything right now, but kissing Pierce. Ever since she'd met him she'd made all the advances, he'd done all the retreating. Even a fool would know she was setting herself up for disappointment here, but she couldn't stop herself.

Part of her longing was based on physical attraction, but there was a huge emotional element, too. A connection that she couldn't explain.

When she looked into his eyes she felt as if she could see his soul. And it was a beautiful thing. Strong, honest and more sensitive than he would ever allow anyone to believe.

Above all she trusted the man, because over and over he had proved to her that he would put her interests ahead of his own.

She wondered if he'd ever been able to rely on anyone to do the same for him.

She touched the hard bulk of his shoulder beneath the thin cotton of his black T-shirt. Ran her fingers through the dark softness of his wavy hair. Pressed her lips against the lightly stubbled plane of his jaw.

If he really didn't want to kiss her, he would have to be the one to pull away.

But he didn't.

And she was so glad about that. Slowly she touched her lips to his. Leaned in closer. Angled her head.

He kissed her back, generating within her body the sort of animal heat that she'd only read about. Where had these primal instincts come from? The urge to devour him, if possible. Be devoured in return. Kisses were not going to be enough. Not nearly enough.

"Georgia…"

She was practically in his lap, but that was what he wanted, wasn't it? She couldn't be the only one feeling this incredible, overpowering desire to crawl into one another's skin.

"Georgia, you're going to have to leave. I can't take this anymore."

She did stop then. Looking into his eyes, she couldn't believe he meant what he said.

"Don't you want to—?"

"Hell, yes, I want to! But, Georgia. You've got to see how impossible this is. I can't seduce you."

"I thought *I* was seducing *you*."

"And you're too damn good at it by far. Just what did that farm boy from South Dakota teach you anyway?"

What Craig had taught her, what they had taught each other, didn't bear any relation to what had just transpired between her and Pierce. They were still close enough that she could feel the quick in and out of his breath on her cheek. Feel his body heat warming her flesh.

She laid a hand on the side of his cheek.

"Pierce, I have hours before I need to leave for work."

He groaned at the implied invitation. "Maybe so. But I need to get my feet on level ground right now." He tore himself from her, all the while watching her distrustfully as if she were a potentially flammable substance.

"What's so great about level ground?" She smoothed down her hair, refusing to feel embarrassed. So she'd thrown herself at the man. So he'd rejected her. Again. She knew he didn't mean it.

"Nothing's great about level ground," Pierce admitted. "But at least I know where I stand. Come on," he held out a hand to her, "let me drive you home."

"I WANT TO GET MARRIED," Reid said. They were in Sylvie's bed, watching a movie together, sipping wine.

"Pardon me?" She couldn't have heard that right.

"I said I want to get married."

Sylvie reached for the remote control and powered off the television. "Reid, you *are* married."

"You know what I mean. I want to divorce *her.* Then marry you."

He'd never spoken this way before. "But your family…"

"Kids survive divorce. Mine will, too." He put an arm around her back and pulled her close. "Don't you want to marry me?"

So many times she'd resented the limitations inherent in dating a married man. But she'd never seriously believed he would leave them for her.

Probably he wouldn't. Probably he was just speaking impulsively right now.

"Divorce would mean a terrible upheaval," she said carefully. "Not just for your children. Have you thought through how it would affect your life? And hers?"

She could feel Reid's body tense. "What are you saying? You don't want me to leave my wife?"

"No, that's not right. I just want to make sure you've thought this through." She also wanted to protect herself. If she got her hopes up, and Reid changed his mind, that would be more painful than if he'd never raised the possibility of committing himself to her.

"I've been thinking about this for weeks. Of course, I don't want to hurt my family. But if I'm miserable in my marriage, what choice do I have?"

"I don't think I can answer that one for you."

Reid got up and paced the width of her bedroom. She could see how agitated he was, and that gave her hope. Hope that he really might leave his wife. Hope that he really did love her enough to get married.

But was she just deluding herself?

She knew very little about his past. Or his present. Or what he wanted for his future for that matter. When they were together, they rarely talked about subjects other than movies they watched together or events in the nightly news broadcast.

She didn't even know the names of his children.

"I'm sure this is the right thing," Reid muttered. "I'll tell Moira this weekend. Maybe I should call my lawyer first—there may be a protocol I need to follow. With any luck, I can be moved in with you by Monday."

Monday. Oh, my lord, Monday. Sylvie felt a shot of exhilaration that was equal parts delight and apprehension.

"Wait a minute, Reid. We need to think very carefully about this. Once you tell Moira, there'll be no turning back." She watched his face carefully, and felt a pang when she spotted hesitation. But it faded quickly.

"What you're saying makes sense. But I want to be with you so badly."

"We have our nights together. Our Sunday mornings."

"It isn't enough, Sylvie."

And it was no longer enough for her, either, she realized suddenly. "Give this a week," she counseled her lover. "Or maybe we should wait until after Christmas."

"No. I couldn't stand to spend Christmas with my family when I'm in love with you. I'd feel like such a hypocrite."

Sylvie understood all too well, and she admired him for wanting to end the deception. They'd started this affair as a romantic lark. Neither had expected their relationship to turn so intense. It had happened so quickly.

Too quickly? She needed to give this some serious thought, as well. Was she sure she wanted to spend the rest of her life with this man?

On the other hand, what was so wonderful about her existing life that she didn't need a change? She was thirty; it was time to settle down. She'd always assumed a husband and kids would be part of her future.

Maybe that husband would be Reid. Maybe those kids would be theirs.

"JACK'S WAITING on line three," Larry said from the control room.

Georgia paused before taking the call. Could Jack

really be her stalker? Was he the one who had broken into her house last night?

A part of her actually hoped he was. Jack didn't sound at all dangerous or violent to her. If he was leaving the flowers, she was sure he meant her no harm.

She queued up the next song, then removed her headphones. She gazed through the glass that divided her from her producer. Surely Larry would let her know if he had sensed anything strange about Jack tonight. But Larry pretended not to see the question in her eyes. After another brief pause, Georgia picked up the phone.

"Jack? What's new?"

"Hi, Georgia. I've been watching a lot of movies lately."

"That sounds like fun. Seen anything good?"

"A couple were okay. I dunno if you'd like them. I seem to be obsessed with dying lately."

Georgia's first reaction was mild shock. Then she told herself not to be ridiculous. "I guess a lot of guys your age are into action flicks, aren't they?"

"I'm not talking about anything really violent or gory. I just want to watch movies where one of the main characters dies. Like *Philadelphia*. Have you seen it?"

"The movie where Tom Hanks's character dies of AIDS. Yes, I've seen it. Jack, you don't—"

"I'm also really into that movie about the kid who's shot at the end—*Pay It Forward*. That's really awesome."

Awesome? "Jack, has something bad happened with Courtney?"

"Nah. She's just ignoring me, like usual. Can you play me a song, Georgia? Something kind of sad and like, mournful?"

"You know what? Maybe you shouldn't listen to any more sad songs tonight. You need something that will lift your spirits."

"You mean drugs?"

"No! I mean do something fun. Do you play any sports?"

"I'm not exactly the most coordinated guy in the world."

"Well, how about going dancing? Or just hanging out with friends?"

"I'd rather talk to you. You're the only one who cares about me. The only…"

"Jack?"

"…one who understands how I feel—"

She glanced at the time and saw she had one and a half minutes before the song that was currently playing would end. "Jack, please, you've got to listen to me. I'm worried about you. I want you to get some help. Do you belong to a church?"

She heard him give a strangled laugh. "Not anymore."

"Well, how about the school guidance counselor?"

"That old bitch? It's *you* I want to talk to. You're the only one."

"But I don't have the time or the training to help you. Instead of talking to me you should be getting some real help." She'd have to ask Larry to screen his calls, Georgia realized, disheartened. For the good of both of them.

"Talk to someone in your family you trust," she pleaded.

"There is no one."

"What about someone at school? If you don't like the guidance counselor maybe there's a teacher you get along with?"

In her zeal to help Jack, she'd lost track of her timing. Larry's voice interrupted the call.

"Georgia, are you there? I've cut that last caller off and put on a jingle."

"Thanks, Larry." She took a deep breath, trying to compose herself.

The jingle ended, and she was on the air. "This is Georgia and you're listening to *Seattle after Midnight*. If you liked that last song I guarantee you'll enjoy this one, too."

Without further introduction, she started the recording next on her play list, not even noticing the name of the song or the artist.

Avoiding Larry's censorious look, she brushed

her curls off her forehead and noticed her skin was damp with sweat. She was really worried about Jack. His problems were deep, way too deep for a DJ to handle.

If only he would reach out to someone. Unless…maybe he had? Were those roses his way of trying to establish a closer relationship with her?

Georgia took a sip of her hot chocolate. She had to get control of her emotions. She had a show to do. She couldn't let Jack's problems preoccupy her. After tonight's show, she would ask Larry not to put through *any* of his calls. Maybe if he couldn't talk to her, he would reach out to someone else. A family member. A trusted teacher.

That was one possibility. Another, Georgia feared, was that Jack would just get more angry and increasingly unstable. If he was the one sending her the roses, that would definitely be a bad thing.

AFTER HER SHOW Georgia had been asleep for about six hours, when she heard a knock at her door. Pierce was anxious to follow up on yesterday's break-in.

"We need to talk to Fred about the key and the security code," he reminded her. He glanced down at her bare feet. "Cute toes."

She curled them under, ridiculously self-conscious considering that her robe covered the rest of her body quite thoroughly. "Maybe you could have called first?"

He ignored that suggestion as he handed her a cup

of coffee in a take-out cup. "Here's breakfast. Let's go see Fred."

"Gee, thanks." Georgia pushed a strand of hair out of her eyes before taking a sip. Vanilla latte. That was nice. "Could I get dressed first?"

"Make it quick. We've got a lot of ground to cover and I have a four o'clock appointment." He sounded annoyed, almost angry.

"If you're busy, why don't you get back to work? I didn't ask for your help. I'm capable of getting my locks changed. And the police are coming over later this afternoon."

"That's good. But not enough." He took the coffee out of her hands. "Now, would you please go upstairs and get some clothes on?"

Or else what? She was tempted to ask. But she didn't. Instead she raced up the stairs and put on a pair of jeans and a pretty pink top, one with flared sleeves and a triangle of lace at the chest.

If Pierce was determined to protect her, she might as well look pretty.

But once she was back downstairs, she felt she might as well be wearing a baseball uniform for all the notice Pierce took.

"Okay, here's your coffee back. Let's go pay Fred a visit."

Her neighbor was stringing Christmas lights across the railing of his porch. As they approached, he plugged in the strand of white fairy lights.

"Getting into the Christmas spirit, Fred?" Georgia asked.

"Why not? Besides, working out here gives me an excuse to watch for that guy I saw hanging around a while ago. Say, I have an extra strand of lights I could hang from your porch if you'd like."

"That would be great, Fred."

"Seen anyone suspicious so far?" Pierce asked.

"Not today. But if I do…" Fred pulled a pair of sport binoculars from the roomy pocket of his coat, "I'm prepared this time. I'll get the plate numbers for sure."

"Good thinking," Pierce said. "Especially since someone broke into Georgia's house when she was doing her Monday night show."

"What?" Fred's weathered eyes flashed in Georgia's direction. "When was this? Georgie-girl are you okay?"

"I wasn't home at the time. All he did was leave me a flower and a note."

"He didn't have to break in to do that. He could have left his delivery with me. I was home all day."

"I'm afraid this guy may not be mentally stable," Pierce said. "What's puzzling me, though, is how he got in and out of Georgia's place when her doors were locked and her alarm was on."

"Good question, young man. Do you think this could be the character I noticed hanging around earlier?"

"I wouldn't be surprised. In the meantime, we need to see where you keep Georgia's spare key."

"Sure thing." Fred set his binoculars on the wicker rocker, then ushered them both inside his house. "It's in the kitchen. Georgie, you lead the way."

She knew the house well, not just because she'd been inside so many times, but also because the floor plan was the mirror to her own. In the kitchen she went straight to the phone mounted on the wall next to a calendar from a real estate agent who kept trying to get Fred to put his house up for sale. There were some hooks in the wall here, too, where Fred hung his own sets of house and car keys.

But she didn't see the key with the KXPG tag that she'd given Fred a couple of weeks after she'd moved in.

"Missing?" Pierce guessed.

"Yes. Fred, is there some other place you might have put the key for safekeeping?" Observing his stricken face, she could tell there wasn't.

"Look at this." Pierce pointed to a piece of paper taped on the wall next to the phone. It contained a list of phone numbers. Right there, next to her name, was Georgia's four-numeral security code.

No secret, now, how her house had been broken into.

CHAPTER NINE

"POOR FRED. He feels so guilty. But he shouldn't. I never told him I had a stalker. Why should he have thought there was any reason to be extra careful?" Georgia put a piece of bread into her toaster, then raised her eyebrows at Pierce, silently asking if he wanted any, too.

Pierce shook his head no. "I agree it's not the old guy's fault, but you still need to get your locks changed."

She had that covered. "I've called a locksmith. He's scheduled me for later this afternoon."

"Well call him back and cancel. I'll change them for you."

"This is the middle of a workweek. I'm sure you have more pressing business than changing my locks."

"I already told you. December's a slow month."

"Right. What about that four o'clock appointment you mentioned earlier?"

"It isn't four o'clock yet, is it? Come on, Georgia. Let me change the locks. It'll make me feel better. Besides, do you have any idea what a locksmith will charge?"

She thought of the estimate she'd received over the phone and hoped the guy would take a credit card.

"See, you're frowning already," Pierce said, seizing his advantage. "I've already bought what I need. It'll take me less time to install the new locks than it would to take them back to the store."

Georgia turned to her toast, which had just popped up. She placed it on a plate and began to cover it with peanut butter. "I don't know what to say. You're being far too generous."

"It's not such a big deal," he insisted.

"Okay. Install the new locks. But you've got to let me make you lunch when you're done."

"If that's the price I've got to pay…."

He left the room to go to his car. Georgia leaned against the counter and watched after him, arms folded over her chest.

There he went again, trying to take care of her. Putting her needs ahead of his own.

No wonder she was falling in love with him.

PIERCE HAD JUST LEFT to borrow a special type of drill head from Fred, who had a well-stocked workshop in his toolshed in the backyard, when Georgia heard a knock at the front door.

She hurried to the entryway and peered out to the

porch. A uniformed police officer stood outside her door. He looked to be in his late thirties, tall and lanky with a bit of gray showing at his temples. She swung the door open.

"Hi. I'm Georgia Lamont."

"Are you kidding? You're that DJ on the radio, aren't you? The one from *Seattle after Midnight.* I'd recognize your voice anywhere."

Georgia smiled. There was something very nice about being recognized. Made the city seem like a smaller, friendlier place, somehow. "That's right."

The officer nodded. "Sergeant Richard London." He showed her his identification. "May I come in?"

"Of course." She stepped back leaving him room to enter. "Let's talk in the living room. Someone's changing my locks for me in the kitchen."

"That's a wise precaution after a break-in. Any idea how the perpetrator got into your house? I see you have a security system. Was it activated at the time?"

"Yes. We're pretty sure he stole my key and the code for my security system from my next-door neighbor." Georgia explained the situation in more detail.

The sergeant asked more questions and made careful note of all her responses.

"According to the report you gave over the phone, no valuables were taken. Is that right?"

She nodded. "Nothing was stolen or damaged.

But he left something behind for me. A rose." She showed London the note that had been left with it. Then explained about the other roses and notes.

"I don't like the sound of this." London shook his head.

She examined the officer more closely. From the moment they'd introduced themselves, her memory had been prodding her about something. "Did you say your name was Richard London?"

"That's right."

"I was doing some research recently… Were you one of the officers who was interviewed by the *Seattle Times* about Cassandra Harding's fatal collision?"

London was visibly taken aback. "That was a couple of years ago."

"I suppose this will strike you as some coincidence, but the man changing my locks for me is Pierce Harding."

"Now there's a name I haven't heard in a while."

"Did you work together?"

"Yeah. We worked on a lot of cases together. "How's he doing? I know his business is thriving. I give him all the referrals I can and I'm not the only one."

Georgia recalled the impeccable offices, the staff she hadn't expected to find. "Yes, his business is doing very well."

"How about his personal life? Has he remarried?"

"No."

"Sorry to hear that. I was hoping that maybe you and he…"

"I'm just a friend."

The officer leaned back in his chair. "Well friends are good, right? Is he still brooding over his wife's accident? He had a hard time dealing with that, not that I blame him. Bloody awful that was."

"Yes."

"I tried to stay in contact with Harding after he left the force, but he made it pretty clear he wasn't interested in keeping ties with his old life."

"His wife's accident scarred him badly. Do you have any theories on why Cassandra would have been driving on the wrong side of the road?"

"We were never able to say for sure, though everyone involved in the collision investigation had their pet theory. In the final analysis, I don't think it really matters. Accidents happen and you just have to accept that fact sometimes. But for Pierce, Cassandra's death was just the final blow. Has he told you about his childhood?"

"Are you kidding? When pressed he admitted he was born in New York City. That was it."

London chuckled. "Yeah, he isn't much on sharing, is he? But we worked together for many years and I know the bare outlines. Both his folks were alcoholics. He had a younger brother, and he tried to look out for him, but the kid was killed in a stupid accident in a shopping mall parking lot. This happened just before Pierce turned sixteen."

What a contrast to her own childhood. No wonder Pierce had listened to her stories about South Dakota as if she were telling him fairy stories.

"He always said Cassandra was the first good thing to happen in his life. Personally, I thought she treated him more like a do-good project than a husband. Still, he was devoted to her and I wasn't at all surprised he took her death so hard." London sighed.

Georgia was so into London's reminiscing, that she started at the sound of the back door closing.

"Georgia?" Pierce called out.

"I'm in the living room. A police officer is here taking my statement."

"Oh?" Pierce came through the hall, wiping his hands on an old rag Georgia had given him earlier. He paused when he spotted the sergeant. "London?"

"Small world, isn't it?" Richard London stood, holding out his hand. "How are you keeping, Harding?"

"Not bad." Pierce shook his hand, his expression a mixture of pleasure and incredulity. His gaze shifted to Georgia. "Has she explained the situation to you?"

"Yeah. This guy sounds like a wacko."

"No kidding." Piece settled on a chair across from London. The two men began to discuss the case in earnest and Georgia mostly listened. In the end, though, London had to agree that there wasn't much the police could do to protect her. Pierce had already covered the basic security measures and there was little chance that attempting to lift fingerprints from the notes would lead to any success.

After London left, Pierce finished with the locks. Georgia made him a sandwich, which he ate standing up at the sink.

"I have to hurry to make that appointment," he explained, washing up when he was done at her sink.

"I have a meeting, too, with my program director." They usually tried to get together every week.

"What's his name again?" Pierce dried his hands on a dishtowel.

"Mark Evans."

"He's the one who heard your program while he was on holiday with his kids, right?"

"Yes. I owe my job to Mark." She crossed her fingers in the air. "Here's hoping he's still happy he hired me."

CANDACE, the daytime receptionist at KXPG, welcomed Georgia with a smile.

"Looking for Mark?" she guessed. "He's in his office."

Georgia found him with his head lowered over a mound of paperwork. Though his office was a disaster, the photographs of his daughter and son were clearly visible amid the chaos.

"Mark, do you have a minute?"

"Georgia." He raised his head and smiled, making her feel welcome.

The program director was good-looking in a boy-next-door sort of way. She'd felt a twinge of interest when she'd first met him, but the fact that he was her boss had been enough to stifle that. For Mark's part, if he found her attractive in return, he was too much of a professional to show it.

"Come on in and sit down. How are you doing? Ratings are great," he rushed to reassure her. "Our advertisers couldn't be happier. Same goes for the general manager."

Her spirits lifted at the good news. "I'm glad to hear that."

"I've got even better news. There's some interest in your program in Oregon. A few of the stations have approached me about the possibility of syndication. What do you say about that?"

She grinned. This was her dream come true.

"It's still early in the negotiation process, but I think your show is a real winner. And trust me, Oregon is just the beginning. How are things working out between you and Larry? Do you like working with him?"

She hesitated for a beat, before nodding. "He knows what he's doing."

"Yeah, Larry's had a lot of experience. And how's the time slot suiting you? Midnight to five must be a little grueling."

"I've always been a night person. The odd hours don't really bother me." Except they did make it difficult to meet people and build a new life. But she wasn't going to complain to Mark Evans about that. He'd offered her the opportunity of a career and she intended to make the most of it.

"Sounds like you have something in common with my daughter." He glanced at the photo on his desk, of a pretty girl with dark-lashed eyes. "She's a night owl, too. Though getting her to bed at a decent hour is turning out to be the least of my problems. She's fifteen this month and figures she ought to be allowed to date."

Georgia liked the way he discussed his family with her so easily. He made her feel like more than just an employee. "Are you going to let her?"

"I'm not sure. What did your parents say when you were that age?"

She tried to remember. "I think I was sixteen before I was allowed to go on a date where it was just me and a guy. But to tell you the truth, I had an unofficial boyfriend long before that and we found plenty of ways to be alone together."

Mark's sigh was despondent. "Yeah, I kind of figure that's going on in our situation, too." He gave her another smile, this one forced where the other had been so natural. "Anyway, the joys of parenthood are something you don't have to worry about. Just keep up the great work on the airwaves and that'll be one less thing I have to concern my-self with."

She'd been on the verge of confiding the details about her stalker. Now she decided against it. The poor guy had enough on his plate. Besides, there wasn't anything he could do about the problem.

She left Mark's office and went to check her mail slot. Another woman was doing the same thing. When she turned, Georgia recognized Rachel Mas-terson. She was taller than Georgia and more slen-der. In her tailored suit and silk blouse she looked very polished and professional.

"Hi, Rachel." After her experiences with Larry, she expected to be ignored or rebuffed in some way. But Rachel sent her a cheery smile.

"Hey there, Georgia. How are you doing? I love your show."

Taken aback by the woman's friendliness, Geor-gia didn't know what to say at first. After a second, she managed to blurt out, "You've listened to my show?"

"Not often I admit." Rachel laughed easily. "I'm not what you'd call a night person, 10:00 p.m. is pretty late for me, so you can see why I'm happy with my new assignment."

She was? That wasn't the impression Larry had given her. "What assignment is that?"

"The slot after the morning show. Mark wants to start a new talk show with a mixture of guests and phone-in callers. We'll be discussing current affairs with a slant toward local Seattle happenings. Isn't that fabulous?"

Georgia remembered Monty telling her that Rachel was gregarious and outspoken. "Actually that does sound pretty good."

"It's exactly what I want. I'm going to call my show *All Things Considered.* What do you think?"

"Good name. Indicates an open mind and a willingness to listen to other people's points of view."

Rachel grinned. "To be honest, I'm not always so good at that. But I'm sure going to try. You know, we should go for coffee sometime. I could fill you in on all the hot gossip about this place."

"I'd love to."

"What about now? The coffee shop next door is handy."

AT THE LITTLE café where Georgia had sat with Pierce the first night they met, Rachel ordered a sweetened coffee and two glazed donuts. "I'm one of those lucky people who can eat anything," she confessed.

Georgia guessed the slender woman burned the extra calories with her huge output of energy. Rachel practically radiated an electrical charge—even when sitting drinking coffee and eating donuts.

"Have you had a chance to get to know many people at the station yet?" Rachel asked.

"I probably know the nighttime security guard better than anyone."

"Monty." Rachel nodded. "He's new, right? I've only spoken to him a few times. I saw the picture of his wife he keeps on his desk. It's so sad what happened to her."

"Yes. I think he must be very lonely. He always seems grateful when I take the time to talk to him."

"That's nice. You've probably heard about Mark, huh? His separation and all that?"

"Well, I know he is separated."

"Oh, it was heartbreaking, let me tell you. I think Jocelyn must have been crazy. I mean, Mark is one of the good ones. You don't toss out a man like that just because you've landed a great job offer. And it's not as if he wouldn't have followed her to Boston. Mark's great at what he does. He could have picked up a position anywhere they have radio waves. But Jocelyn didn't even give him a chance."

"What does she do?"

"She's an English professor. She was offered a position at Harvard," Rachel added casually.

"Wow. Well, that is impressive."

"Yeah, it's great and all that, but do you think any job is worth leaving your husband? Abandoning your kids?"

"Surely she didn't abandon them."

"She saw them two weeks last summer. And she's planning to take them to Hawaii the week after

Christmas. That's it, as far as I can tell." Rachel licked a smudge of icing from her lips. "Anyway, I feel really sorry for Mark. I hope he finds a good woman soon, but he works such long hours, then has to go home and take care of his kids. How's he going to meet someone with a schedule like that?"

Georgia was doubly glad she hadn't told Mark about the stalker. Should she tell Rachel? She decided to ease into the subject. "I'm glad you're happy with your new assignment. From a few things my producer said, I was afraid you might be annoyed at me for taking your time slot."

"Larry said that?" Rachel took a sip of coffee. "What an idiot. He's the one who was upset at the change, not me."

"He called you his girlfriend."

Rachel hooted. "Did he really? Well, we did go out a few times. Working late every night together, one thing led to another and before I knew it, Larry was getting serious. I was doubly glad about the reassignment because it gave me an excuse to break off with him."

Georgia chuckled. "I can see I should have gone out for coffee with you as soon as I moved here."

"You're absolutely right about that. If you ever need the scoop at KXPG, I'm the one to come talk to. Now tell me about you. Where'd you come from and how did you cultivate that fabulous radio presence?"

"Well, I'm from South Dakota."

"Oh, that's right. I remember Mark talking about being stuck in that hotel in Sioux Falls with Shane barfing every fifteen minutes, poor kid."

"That must have been so awful. Still, I guess it's lucky for me that Shane did get sick."

"Mark was very impressed when he heard your show. We've all been impressed with what you've done since you came to Seattle. And now that I've met you—" Rachel's green eyes narrowed on Georgia in an assessing manner "—I have to say you're a very intriguing person. On air you sound so sophisticated and sultry. Yet in person you seem more down-home and…sweet."

"So I've been told." Georgia thought of how surprised Pierce had been when he'd met her. "I didn't consciously set out to invent a separate radio persona. I can't explain why I'm so different on the air from real life."

"I think both are the real Georgia. That's what makes you so interesting. And it also explains why you relate so well to your audience. Something I just couldn't do when I had that time slot. My mother always says I'm like a bull in a china shop and she's so right. I can't stop myself from saying what I think."

Georgia agreed with her assessment, and liked Rachel all the more for her frankness. "I predict your phone-in talk show is going to be very successful."

Rachel's smile showed her pleasure. "I think we've both found our niches, Georgia. The Seattle airwaves are never going to be the same!"

AFTER CHANGING Georgia's locks, Pierce met with his client as planned, then put in several hours at the office. By eight o'clock, though, he'd lost his ability to concentrate. He decided to go for a drive. By coincidence, his drive took him by Georgia's house.

Well, now that he was here, he might as well do a routine check of the neighborhood.

Between her new security system and the old guy next door, he shouldn't have had reason to worry. But Pierce couldn't seem to stop himself. Lately Georgia was in his thoughts at all hours of every day. If he wasn't careful, his business would start to suffer. He couldn't continue to pile all the extra duties on Jake's and Will's shoulders.

Lights were on at Georgia's house and he ended up stopping and getting out of his car. As he stepped up to the porch he could smell something baking. All of a sudden an old memory assailed him. His mother had never spent much time in the kitchen. She had rarely cooked anything beyond opening a can or using a toaster. But on one of his birthdays—he thought it was probably the sixth—she'd gotten it into her head that she was going to make him a birthday cake.

He remembered the rich, sweet scent, wafting in

the apartment that afternoon, and his own excitement that he was going to have a real birthday cake.

But his mother had been steadily drinking all afternoon and when it came time to ice the cake, she just couldn't do it. The cake had come out of the oven lopsided. The icing she'd made was too thick and it hardened before she had time to spread it. He remembered her laying her head on the counter as she sobbed and sobbed, his younger brother, Jay, pulling on her pant leg and crying, too. That day Pierce had wished he'd never been born. Then his mother wouldn't have needed to bake that stupid cake.

Now why had his mind dredged up that particular memory? Pierce wiped his shoes dry on Georgia's welcome mat, then rang the doorbell.

It took a minute for the door to open.

"Pierce." Georgia looked surprised to see him, but pleased.

As he stepped inside, he wished just walking into her home didn't feel so damn wonderful. Music played in the background and the baking aroma enveloped him like a warm hug.

A guy could get used to this, he thought, before he remembered that he'd tried domesticity once, and actually he hadn't been able to get used to it.

"So, do you still have a job?" he asked, referring to her earlier meeting with her boss.

Her smile widened. "I do. In fact there's good

news." A timer sounded and Georgia put up her hand. "Just a minute, I have to get something from the oven."

He followed her to the kitchen where she removed a tray of cookies, replacing it with another one dotted with mounds of raw dough.

She told him about the syndication offer from Oregon, the high ratings, her conversation with Rachel Masterson.

"Sounds like you had a good afternoon. What time are you planning to leave to go to the station tonight?"

"Around eleven."

"Will you let me drive you? And pick you up when the show is over?"

He saw the relief in her eyes and knew she'd been worried about the stalker.

"I hate to let you to do that," she said. "When will you sleep?"

"Most nights I stay up to listen to your show anyway."

She passed him a cookie from a tray on the table and he took a bite. It had oatmeal and chocolate and just the right amount of crunch.

"Good," he mumbled, around the crumbs in his mouth.

"Monty's favorite. I'm going to take him a big tinful."

No doubt she'd take some of the cookies to her

neighbor as well. He wondered if Georgia had found people to take care of in South Dakota, too. Probably. They must miss her like hell.

"Would you like something to drink with that? I'm having milk, but I could make you some coffee."

"No, no, that's okay. I really should go for a run, I haven't exercised in days. How about I come back in a couple of hours. Will that get you to work on time?"

She nodded, but her gaze seemed uncertain. What was bothering her, he wondered. The time? Or his refusal to stay and have a drink?

She saw him out and at the door he was tempted to change his mind. The run had just been an excuse to leave, though it was a good idea. With Georgia he couldn't seem to find the right balance. Protecting her from the stalker without getting too close to her himself.

"You don't have to go, you know." She leaned against the door frame, her eyes warm with invitation.

She'd never looked sexier to him. Or more lovable.

"Pierce?"

"Yeah?"

"Are you ever going to ask me out?"

He froze for a second, startled, then impressed. She didn't play games. He liked that. Among many other things about her.

"I don't know," he answered honestly. "If I did, would you say yes?"

She made him wait a few beats for her answer. When it came, it was ambiguous. "Maybe. If you're lucky."

She closed the door before he could tell her that that was the problem. He wasn't lucky. Not at all.

PIERCE RETURNED later to pick up Georgia as promised. He'd used his time, not to go for the run after all, but to start a couple of background checks. Georgia kept insisting her stalker was Jack, but Pierce was worried about the people closer to home. Those were the ones who had the easiest access to her, and therefore the most power to hurt her. He wanted to know as much as possible about them.

They drove in silence to the KXPG offices. He stopped by the main entrance, getting out of the car in order to walk her inside.

"Thanks for the ride, Pierce." Georgia paused at the doors, expecting him to leave, but he entered the building with her. Monty Greenfield, the security guard, was one of the people he was running a background check on. He wanted a chance to meet the man in person.

Monty was sitting behind the security desk as they entered the building. He was a slightly rotund man with thinning hair and bushy eyebrows. Pierce guessed he was in his early fifties.

The security guard glanced up at them, showing obvious surprise at seeing Pierce with Georgia.

"Hey, Monty. This is Pierce Harding, a friend of mine. And I brought you some cookies." Georgia handed the older man the large tin Pierce had seen earlier in her kitchen.

"Are they my favorites?" Monty cracked open the lid, then smiled. "You're the best, Georgia."

"I hope you enjoy them."

Pierce watched the interplay with interest. While Georgia was just being kind, Monty clearly adored her. Could he be her so-called "secret admirer"?

"I've got to run upstairs," Georgia said. She patted Monty's arm, then nodded at Pierce. "Thanks again for the lift."

"My pleasure." He waited until she'd left. "Nice woman, huh?"

"Georgia's terrific. How do you know her?" His gaze was more than a little curious.

"We met through my work," Pierce said, purposefully ambiguous. "Say, did you hear what happened with the Sonics last night?"

He and Monty talked basketball for a while. When that conversation died, Pierce pointed at the photograph on Monty's desk. "Is that your wife? Georgia told me you lost her a while ago. Sorry to hear that."

"Yeah, it was rough."

Pierce was about to ask another question when Georgia burst back into the reception area.

She didn't need to say a word for him to comprehend the problem. In her arms were roses. Three of them.

CHAPTER TEN

"THEY WERE IN my studio," Georgia said, holding out the roses to Pierce.

As he took them from her hands, anger welled inside Pierce, along with a sense of helplessness. This guy kept getting to Georgia, no matter what he did.

"Show me," he said.

Georgia nodded, then headed for the open stairs behind the security desk. Pierce followed her to the third story where her studio was tucked into the far northwest corner. He hung back at the doorway while she slipped ahead and settled into her chair. He hadn't imagined her studio like this. He'd always pictured her in a cozy room of romantic ambiance.

In reality, her studio was brightly lit and filled with equipment. The room was about fifteen square feet, with two windows. One faced out to the central newsroom where he was now standing, the other to her producer's control room.

Georgia sat facing the second window. Three computer monitors were placed at intervals along her desk. Front and center was a control panel with lots of dials and knobs and levers. Two fat microphones were suspended on metal folding arms on either side of the control panel.

On the wall opposite from Georgia's desk sat a small table and two chairs, and against the connecting wall, a tower of electronic equipment stood next to a metal filing cabinet.

Finished his quick survey of the space, he glanced back at Georgia. "Where did you find the roses?"

"On my keyboard." She pointed.

"I'm guessing no one was around to see who did it?"

"No. The newsroom is deserted at this hour of night. And Larry hasn't shown up to work, yet."

"I don't like this." Pierce strode into the room, then stopped, frustrated. "This guy is taking bigger and bigger risks. And we still don't have a clue who he is."

"Only someone who worked in this building would have been able to get past security to my studio."

Their gazes held for a moment.

"That lets out Jack," she said soberly.

He glanced back at the panel door dividing her studio from the newsroom. Checking the handle, he asked, "Do you ever lock this?"

"I haven't. No one does around here." Her gaze shied away from the roses he still carried. "Could you do me a favor and throw those away?"

He nodded, understanding why she wouldn't want them around. Their perfume alone would be a constant reminder that her studio had been invaded now, as well as her home.

"Have you read the note?" He could see the paper still wrapped around one of the stems.

"I can't. Not now, not before my show." She sat stiffly in her chair, her shoulders tight, her jaw clenched.

God, he'd love to catch this jerk. Did he have any idea how badly he was frightening her?

Pierce stilled at the sound of a door opening down the hall, then muffled footsteps on carpet. Larry Sizemore appeared in the doorway. He put a hand on his neatly trimmed goatee and eyed Pierce cautiously.

While Georgia introduced the two men, Pierce had the opportunity to size up the producer. He was smartly dressed in a black turtleneck and black slacks, carrying a trench coat slung over one arm, and a briefcase in his other hand. He looked attractive, stylish…and very unfriendly.

"Sorry, I'm late," he said in a tone that did not sound remorseful at all. "Something came up at the last minute."

"No problem," Georgia said, though her smile appeared strained. She didn't mention the roses, and while Larry's gaze had stopped pointedly at the flowers in Pierce's hand, he didn't say anything about them, either.

"Okay. I'd better get to work." Larry nodded to Pierce, then headed for his own room.

"Friendly guy," Pierce observed quietly, once he and Georgia were alone again.

"Isn't he just?"

"So," Pierce held up the flowers. "I'll get rid of these and hold on to the note. We can take a look at it later."

"Later," she echoed.

As he turned to leave, he glanced back at her one last time. She looked small and vulnerable in her swivel chair, holding a set of headphones as if she had no idea what to do with them.

For a moment it seemed she was about to ask him something, but in the end all she did was shrug.

"Later," he said again before closing the door between them. On the way out, he paused at the window. She'd slipped on her headphones and was adjusting the levers on her control panel.

Seattle after Midnight was about to begin.

IN HIS CAR, Pierce turned on the radio. He'd checked with Monty on his way out and the security guard had assured him no one without security clearance had been in the building.

That narrowed the field of suspects, but not by much. Hundreds of people were employed in that particular five-story building and while Pierce leaned toward the theory that the stalker was someone Georgia knew personally, he had to consider the possibility that he was wrong. Georgia's stalker could be anyone with access to the building. Anyone at all.

Pierce started his car, then turned on his lights and windshield wipers. As he pulled out of the parking lot, Georgia's voice called to him from the radio.

"Welcome to *Seattle after Midnight*. This is KXPG and you're listening to Georgia. Tonight we're talking about love. And about risk. If you've been hurt, give me a call and tell me what it would take to make you love again."

Pierce sucked in a breath. It felt for all the world as if she were sitting in the car with him right now, asking him that very question.

What would it take to make you love again?

Did she think he was keeping his distance from her because he was afraid of getting hurt? If only she knew the truth. He wasn't afraid to love again. Because he'd never figured out how to love in the first place.

He switched off the radio and drove the dark, wet streets in silence.

At home he tossed Georgia's roses in the trash after retrieving the note. His stomach rumbled. He hadn't eaten since the sandwich Georgia had prepared for him early that afternoon but he was too exhausted to prepare something or even pour himself a drink.

He sank into the sofa and closed his eyes. After a few minutes, he leaned over to turn on the radio.

The seductive strains of a light-jazz standard made his apartment feel not quite so empty. He sprawled out on the sofa, using Cass's needlepoint pillow as a headrest. The stuffing was stiff; it wasn't very comfortable, but he was too tired to care.

How had he gotten himself tangled in this mess with Georgia? He was discouraged that he hadn't been able to help her. And angry that his failure bothered him so much.

Seeing her quiet desperation tonight had reminded him of the other times he'd failed to help people he cared about.

Cass. He never thought about his former wife without being haunted by the manner of her death. If only he could know, with one-hundred percent certainty, whether he could have prevented her accident in any way. Had problems in their marriage, her dissatisfaction with him, been at the root of her driving error?

Despite having investigated every aspect of her accident, he didn't know.

He didn't know what her state of mind had been that afternoon. He didn't know if she'd been aware she was driving on the wrong side of the road. He didn't even know if she might have seen death as a release from the life she'd chosen to live with him.

Her death was as much a mystery now as it had been the night of the crash. He remembered Richard London trying to tell him after the funeral, "It wasn't anyone's fault—it was just one of those things." And Pierce thinking, "That isn't good enough. There has to be a reason."

"This is Georgia and you're listening to *Seattle after Midnight* on KXPG." Georgia's voice hooked him, pulling him out of his bleak reverie.

"We've got a lot of ground to cover tonight," she said. "Let's start with the modern jazz scene. Lizz Wright is an up-and-comer with a great song about pain. And about overcoming pain. I think you all know what I mean by that. 'Open Your Eyes,' Seattle. Lizz has something to say that you need to hear…."

The song started and Pierce felt the music like a drug, seeping into his bones and damn near making him cry. He closed his eyes, expecting to be assailed, as always, by his guilt about Cass. But instead he felt himself pulled further back, to a memory of his brother.

Jay had been a smiley kid, right from the beginning. Pierce's earliest memories were of his brother grinning at him from the playpen where their mother put him when she began her afternoon "cocktail hour."

Play with me! that grin seemed to be saying, and Pierce wished his memory had him reaching out to his baby brother. But no, he'd ignored the kid most of the time. Even when they were both older, he hadn't bothered to notice that Jay was hanging out with a bad crowd, keeping dangerously late hours and developing even more dangerous habits.

If Cass's death had made no sense, well, neither had Jay's. Kids playing around in an outdoor parking lot. Smoking. Writing graffiti. Getting into trouble. A big truck had begun backing out of a loading dock. One of Jay's buddies issued a dare. The driver had no chance of stopping in time. Stupid. Stupid. Stupid.

He could have saved Jay, if he'd tried. Kept him off the streets. Made sure he went to school. He could have been a better brother, just as he could have been a better husband to Cass.

The song on the radio ended and for one, maybe two seconds there was silence. Then Georgia spoke. "Amazing, isn't she? How many of us are afraid to love? Afraid to fly? If you know what I'm talking about, give me a call. I'd love to hear from you."

Georgia read a poem then, something by Emily Dickinson comparing a person recovering from terrible pain to a person freezing in the snow. She followed that with another song, this one with a melody so tender, he just couldn't stand it.

He sprang from the sofa and turned off the radio. The sudden silence fell on him like a heavy burden. Cass's cushion still in his hand, he wandered his sparsely furnished apartment, almost poured himself a drink, then changed his mind and went across the hall to the office.

Despite explicit orders to the contrary, Robin had decorated the reception area with a sad artificial tree that she'd picked up at a garage sale for five dollars.

The little tree glowed in the darkened space. Someone had forgotten to unplug the lights. He bent for the extension cord, then changed his mind and straightened. Actually, the tree didn't look half-bad now that it was decorated. Will had brought in a box of cast-off ornaments from his house. Apparently this year his wife had switched from their traditional green-and-red color scheme to silver and blue.

God. Thinking of all the ways people found to waste their time and money over the holiday season made his head ache.

He went into his inner office, ran a hand over his desk, then, realizing he still held Cass's pillow, he tossed it on the leather chair in the corner.

It looked surprisingly good there.

The cat stuck her head out of the top filing cabinet drawer, checked out the scene, then pounced to the floor. She arched her back and mewed a greeting.

"Yeah, yeah, leave me alone, would ya?" He turned his back on the cat, and the next thing he knew she'd settled herself on the leather chair, right on top of Cass's pillow.

Bloody cat. She'd get hair all over the pillow. But Pierce didn't shoo her away. Instead, he reached out to the radio on his desk and switched it on.

He was such a fool, but he couldn't resist her. He tried and he tried, but he just couldn't tune her out.

IN HIS DARK BEDROOM, Brady Walsh listened to a female vocalist wondering "Do You Love Me Still," and felt as if the lyrics had been written for him. He'd followed Courtney to her locker today, on the off chance he might catch her attention.

He wasn't sure what he'd hoped would happen. Maybe that she'd say something like, "Too bad we didn't get assigned the science project together." That would have been more than enough to make him happy.

But she hadn't looked at him, hadn't even glanced in his direction. He'd hung back at the water fountain, pretending to take a drink, as she talked to one of her girlfriends.

"So who's your partner for the science project?" Courtney asked her friend.

"Justin Griffith. I'm so happy. He'll end up doing most of the work. And you?"

"Alicia York."

"Oh, she's such a loser."

"Yeah, but better Alicia than Brady Walsh. I worked on a project with him at the beginning of the year and he, like, drooled over me the whole time."

"Brady Walsh? Yuck!"

He'd wiped the water from his face and hurried off in the other direction. He couldn't be positive Courtney knew he'd been listening, but he was ninety-five percent sure. Her way of telling him to back off? Or did she just get a thrill out of being cruel?

Well, he was backing off. Damn Courtney. Damn all the girls at the stupid private school his father had insisted he attend. Did he mind that his son was miserable there? The answer, Brady knew, was no. His father didn't care and he never would.

As for his mother, well, she wanted the best for him, Brady knew, but she just didn't get it.

When he'd come home from school that afternoon she'd been in the kitchen baking cookies. She always baked cookies when she was trying to pretend everything was all right.

"Why don't you invite some friends over this weekend?" she'd suggested in her fake-cheerful voice. "Rent a few movies and order in pizza? That would be fun, wouldn't it?"

He didn't even know what to say when she suggested things like that. How would she react, he wondered, if he told her, "I don't have any friends, Mom. The girls think I'm a geek cause I'm so freakin' ugly. The guys treat me like a loser because my marks are too high."

Well, his marks used to be too high. They weren't anymore. Though math had once been his best subject, he'd barely passed his last quiz.

He didn't care, though. He just didn't care.

The only thing that gave him any pleasure these

days was *Seattle after Midnight*. He didn't understand why Georgia had asked him not to call her anymore. Didn't she like him? He'd been so sure that she was the one person who really got him.

Listening to her program now, he felt as if she'd planned it special for him. For a while he found it comforting to just lie there and listen. Then the door to his mother's room slammed shut. Five minutes later she was sobbing.

Hell! He had to get out of here. Being Brady Walsh was far too painful. He much preferred being Jack.

"I'VE GOT Amanda on the phone," Georgia said. "Amanda, what would it take to make you love again?"

"I'm not sure, Georgia." The woman speaking sounded young and very tentative. "There's a guy at work who's been hinting that he'd like to ask me out, but whenever he brings up the subject I find an excuse to leave the room or I change the subject."

"Don't you like this guy?"

"Oh, I do! But I'm afraid, too. The last time I went through a breakup it hurt so bad. See my boyfriend and I were going to get married. He'd bought me a ring, we'd even sent the invitations. Then I found out he was meeting his ex-girlfriend for lunch every week. He told me it didn't mean anything, and I wanted to believe him, but deep in my heart I knew something was wrong."

"And was it?"

"Three weeks before the wedding he eloped with that girl."

"Oh, honey."

"My friends and family said I was better off without him, but it isn't that simple. What did he see in her that he didn't see in me?"

Georgia felt the pain of the poor caller's insecurity down to her bones, even though she'd never been in that situation herself.

"Don't let one sad experience shake your confidence in yourself. Heartache and rejection happen to all, even the rich and famous. You start dating again, Amanda. And have a good time, okay?"

Georgia turned off the recording button as Larry took over the air for a while with some prerecorded messages. She removed her headphones and grabbed an apple from her stash of food under the table.

She'd found it harder than usual to get into her show tonight—those damn roses had really thrown her. But now that she'd warmed up, things were humming along nicely.

She wondered if Pierce was listening. Just the possibility that he might be kept her in high gear, even when she felt she was flagging. The more she learned about the man, the more she felt she understood his reluctance to get involved with her. How she wished she could convince him to take a flying leap into their relationship, without worrying about the consequences.

If he *was* listening tonight, she hoped he got the message.

SYLVIE TURNED her head and observed Reid's still profile. He'd fallen asleep after their lovemaking again…this seemed to be his new pattern. He was snoring, but the gentle sound was not what was keeping Sylvie awake.

She was torn about the future. Reid had brought a ring with him tonight, and while she wasn't so foolish as to make a life decision based on a pretty bauble, she had to admit the gorgeous diamond—and all it represented—was pretty tempting at four o'clock in the morning.

What would the future hold for her as Reid's wife?

Her inability to answer that question had kept her tossing and turning for hours.

Finally admitting to herself that she was not going to fall asleep any time soon, Sylvie crept out of the bed and went to draw a bath for herself. Once soaking in the fragrant warm water, she turned on the radio and immediately found herself immersed in Georgia's most compelling show yet.

"What would it take to make *you* love again?" Georgia asked. "What's holding you back? Let's listen to a woman in Bellevue who thinks she's made a big mistake…."

Sylvie's interest peaked as the woman on the line

spoke of an illicit affair. When Georgia expressed a combination of sympathy and caution, Sylvie wondered what Georgia would say if *she* called the program and confessed her own dilemma with Reid.

Would Georgia advise her to leave the man alone because he belonged to someone else? Or would she suggest Sylvie grasp her shot at happiness while she had the chance?

As always, Sylvie's thoughts drifted to her mother. She had never been one to ram her opinion down her daughter's throat. When Sylvie made a mistake in judgment—as she sometimes had—her mother had offered only loving compassion.

Sylvie had never known a warmer human being.

As the tears gathered in her eyes, she wondered if she would ever get over this intense sense of loss where her mother was concerned. She just couldn't accept that her mother had died. It didn't make sense, didn't feel right. And yet when she'd questioned the doctor he'd said, "These things sometimes happen."

The whole thing was so wrong.

Sylvie stepped out of the tub and wrapped her body in a terry robe. With damp feet, she padded back to bed with Reid. He would be waking soon. She didn't want to waste another precious minute before he left.

PARKED IN THE KXPG lot, Pierce waited for Georgia. Her show had ended twenty-five minutes ago.

He'd turned off the radio and was now sitting in silence. He couldn't help reflecting on some of the things Georgia had said on her show that night, which irritated the hell out of him.

What was the point of his pondering the mysteries of love? That was one case he'd already solved where he was concerned. He was better off steering clear of the whole messy subject.

So why did just spotting Georgia's silhouette at the front entrance of the office building set his heart into a frenzy?

He leaped out of his car and dashed up to the sidewalk, just as Monty was holding the glass door open for Georgia.

"That was some show tonight," the security guard said.

Georgia flushed a little. From the compliment, or because she'd spotted him waiting for her? Pierce stood back as she turned to say goodbye to Monty.

"I'll be fine from here, thanks. You have a good evening, okay?"

"Sure thing." Monty nodded, then receded into the building.

Pierce and Georgia stood for a moment, not speaking, just staring at each other. Pierce had no idea what she saw when she looked at him. But every now and then she just took his breath away.

"Jack didn't call tonight?" Pierce took her arm to walk her to the car—an instinctive gesture that he immediately regretted. Holding her this close made him long for much, much more.

"According to Larry, he tried to get through a couple of times. But I couldn't handle speaking to him. Not after the roses."

Pierce let go of her arm in order to open the car door. Once they were on the road, Georgia started talking again.

"Last time he called, Jack made several references to death. I'm worried he might be suicidal. I'm hoping that if he stops using me and my show as a crutch, he'll get the help he really needs." She sighed. "I don't know what else to do."

"You've got your own problems to deal with," Pierce said. As if she needed reminding.

"Yes. This last bunch makes for a total of nine roses. Only three more and I'll have received the whole dozen." She wrapped her arms around her body and he knew she was wondering, what would happen then?

"What did he say in that first note? 'Then you'll be mine.'"

"I can't believe I ever thought he seemed sweet. Those words sound so sinister to me now."

Pierce agreed. "I think it's significant that he left them in your studio this time. It's like he's telling you there's no place you're safe."

"No kidding. First my car. Then my home. Now my desk."

Pierce pulled up in front of Georgia's house. Both sides of the duplex were dark at this early hour of the morning.

"I'm afraid to go in," she confessed. "I don't want to find any more flowers."

"I'll check out the place for you." He'd been planning to walk her to the door, anyway. Taking her keys from her hand, he strode up the walk, scanning the porch and mailbox before unlocking the front door.

"Input the code, would you?" he asked Georgia, before starting a search of the house. Everything seemed as it should be. He found no flowers in any of the rooms.

"It's secure," he told her as he came down the stairs from her bedroom.

"Thank God." She locked the front door, then sagged against it. "I know this isn't fair of me, but I feel so much safer when you're here."

Did she know how she got to him when she said that? He loved the idea of protecting Georgia. Loved it so much that it scared him. "I have to go out of town on business today."

He needed to follow up some questions that had arisen from the background checks he'd performed on a couple of the people who worked at KXPG. But he didn't tell Georgia this. He knew she'd insist that he bill her for the costs of the flight as well as his time.

No way was he going to do that. Georgia wasn't a client. She was… Well, he didn't know what she was, but she sure as hell wasn't just a name on a file to him.

"Did you read the latest note?" Georgia asked, clearly reluctant to raise the subject.

"Yeah. I've got it with me." He pulled out the piece of paper from his pocket. This one was the worst of all and he wished he didn't have to show her.

Georgia shook her head when he tried to hand it to her. "Read it to me, please."

"It's much longer than usual," he warned. He scanned his eyes over the paragraphs, wondering how he could soften the impact of this. Finally he realized there was no way.

"It's a mock wedding invitation," he said, bluntly. "It begins, 'The honor of your presence is requested at the marriage of Georgia Ann Lamont—'" Pierce glanced up. "Is that your correct full name?"

"It is." She looked appalled. "How could he know that? I don't even broadcast my last name, let alone the middle one."

"There are many ways, if you know where to look. The Internet makes this sort of stuff all too easy to access. Of course, your full name would be in the personnel records at work, too."

Georgia pressed her hand to her mouth.

He scanned the rest of the psycho-invitation. "The name of the groom has been left blank here."

"Oh, God, this is just too sick. Does he give any other details? A date? A location?"

"No, it just says, 'Two hearts united as they were always meant to be.'"

Georgia took the invitation from him. "I feel like burning this."

"You should probably show it to the police. Though I doubt there will be much they can glean from this. He's used stock paper, a standard laser printer. Still, pass this on to them. It can't hurt."

"I will."

"Good." He studied her face, seeing traces of fear, confusion, shock. He wished he could stay to offer the protection she'd told him she needed. "I'm afraid I've got to run for my plane. But you should know I installed a miniature video camera in the roof over your porch. If he comes back to the house, we'll get a picture."

"Do you think he will come back?"

"So far he's never delivered flowers to the same place twice. So let's hope not."

He put a hand on the doorknob, fighting the urge to put his arms around her.

She moved closer to him. "Where are you going?"

"A quick trip to Denver. I'll be back in plenty of time to drive you to work tonight."

"In time for dinner?" Georgia asked, in quiet invitation.

Pierce didn't have the heart to turn her down. "Yes. In time for dinner."

"I could make us something—"

"Why not take a break from the kitchen today. We'll go out."

"Yes," she said quickly. "That would be great."

"Okay. We'll do a late dinner then I'll drive you to the station."

As he finally turned to make his exit, she did her best to give him a carefree smile. But he could spot the worry behind it. He didn't blame her. With only three roses to go, this situation was definitely coming to a head. He could only hope that he'd find out something in Denver that would point him in the right direction to stop it.

CHAPTER ELEVEN

PIERCE WENT HOME to shower, change and collect his papers. Before heading out to the airport, he stopped at the office to check in with Robin. "How are things?"

"Busy as hell." Little stickies completely covered her computer screen. Robin removed one of them and shoved it in his face. "Magnum Securities sent over a file. They want fifteen background checks by next week."

"Give the work to Will."

"He's up to his eyeballs with that personal injury case you gave him last week. He's spoken to several witnesses and the stories don't jive. We could be talking about major damages here."

"Okay, fine. Let Jake do the background checks."

"Has he done them before?"

"He'll figure it out. Anything else?"

Robin surveyed her rainbow of stickies and sighed. "Nothing that can't wait, I suppose. What about on your end? You seem pretty tied up lately. Must be the Lamont case, huh? Want me to do a first billing for you?"

Pierce didn't know how to respond. He wished Georgia had never set foot in his office. Since the rose incident, Robin had been giving him the most annoying, knowing glances. And now this. She *knew* he wasn't going to bill Georgia for anything.

"I guess that means no, huh? Maybe she's paying you in roses?"

Pierce took one of the stickies from her computer, the one that said, 'Get boss to sign payroll checks,' and placed it on the desk in front of her. "Watch your step, Robin, or that's how you'll be paid, too."

Robin immediately straightened in her chair. "Have a good trip to Denver, Mr. Harding."

He nodded in approval. "Now that's more like it."

DESPITE HER growing fears about her stalker, Georgia slept solidly for six hours after Pierce left. When she awoke, she bathed and dressed quickly. The phone rang while she was eating a toasted bagel with cream cheese.

"Georgia? It's Mark. Your show last night really resonated with the people of Seattle. Listeners are still phoning in this morning."

She felt like dancing across the kitchen floor. *Yes!* "That's wonderful, Mark. I had so many calls last night, I was planning to spend a few extra hours in my studio today to cull through them all."

Those she thought would make for good radio she would edit in preparation for tonight's show.

"Well, pop in and say hello when you get here, okay?"

"You bet."

She cleaned up from her breakfast, then got ready to go to the office. After securing her home, she went next door to see how Fred was doing.

The widower invited her inside, telling her proudly, "I've found a safer hiding spot for your key." He opened his freezer and pulled out one of the dinners she'd made for him. Taped to the bottom of the lid was her key. On the piece of masking tape itself, was her four-numeral code.

"Very clever, Fred."

"I just have to remember not to eat this one."

They had a laugh over that, then Georgia left for the station. During the day, the parking lot was almost completely full and she felt much safer walking to the entrance alone than she did at night. She nodded to the daytime security guard, then stopped to chat to the receptionist.

Since she had time to spare, she decided to stock up on office supplies, including some paper for her printer. She was crouched low, with her head inside an open cabinet, when she heard someone join her in the supply room.

She withdrew her head from the cabinet, but with several shelves in the way, she couldn't see who was there. Then someone began to speak and she realized two people, not just one, were in the room with her.

"I don't want to talk here." It was her producer, Larry, speaking in upset but hushed tones. "Can't you at least let me buy you a cup of coffee?"

"No way, Larry. How many times do I have to tell you? I don't want to see you anymore."

Georgia had hesitated just a second too long to announce her presence. Now she decided her best bet was to keep quiet. Hopefully they would both leave before they realized they weren't alone.

"I told you I have plans for this afternoon." Rachel sounded as if her patience had been tested to the limit already.

"But I don't understand what happened between us. Weren't we having a good time together? I think I deserve an explanation for why you want to end things so abruptly."

"Why are you making such a big deal out of this? We saw each other a few times over the course of a couple of months. It was never a serious relationship."

"Maybe not to you."

"Well, I'm sorry. But whatever it was, it's over now. There's nothing else to discuss. And I've got to tell you, if I see you hanging around my apartment one more time, I'm going to make such a big stink you might end up losing your job."

"Rachel!" Larry's anguish was evident in his tone.

"I've got to go. I told you I have plans."

The door opened and Georgia heard footsteps

leading down the corridor. Standing to make her own escape, she discovered, too late, that Larry was still in the supply room.

His eyes rounded at the sight of her, then his mouth twisted in a scowl.

Georgia wanted to deny that she'd heard anything, if only to save Larry's pride. But any claim to that effect would be ludicrous. This was a small room. Of course she'd heard every word.

"I'm sorry, Larry." She didn't know what else to say.

He turned his back on her and stalked out of the room.

Oh, dear. She guessed Larry was going to be even harder to work with after this. She gathered the sheaf of paper she'd come for, then headed for Mark's office. She found him at his desk.

"Georgia. Great to see you."

After Larry's forbidding scowl, it was nice to be greeted by a smile. "How are you doing, Mark?"

"Swamped. But that's the way I like it. I'm glad you could drop in. I can't tell you how thrilled we are by the response you're getting in this city. We've got markets coming begging. So, what do you think about changing the title of your show to *Georgia after Midnight?*

He beamed proudly at her. "We'll launch the new title in January, throw a little party. Sound okay?"

She couldn't keep her smile from spreading wide.

"Will you think I'm horribly egotistical if I admit I've dreamed of this moment since I was in the sixth grade?"

Mark laughed. "I'll think you're human. So let's do it." Abruptly his expression turned sober. "I had a meeting with Larry earlier. He mentioned that one of your callers is getting a little intense. And you've been receiving anonymous gifts?"

"Yes. Roses." She was surprised that Larry had taken the trouble to report this problem to a higher level.

"Is there any extra security we can offer to make you feel safer? I take it your home phone number is unlisted?"

"Yes. And I've recently had a home security system installed."

"Good for you. What about calling the police?"

"I've done that." She told him about the recommendations Richard London had made, basically all of which she was following.

"I guess you're on top of the situation, but if there are any new developments would you please let me know? We want to keep you safe. We have big plans for you here at KXPG."

"I like the sound of that. By the way, how's your daughter doing? Did you make any decisions on when she's allowed to start dating?"

Mark groaned. "Sydney's arranged her first official date for tonight. Which reminds me, I've got to make sure I'm home by five so I can scare the crap out of this guy when he comes to pick her up."

IN DENVER Pierce visited a woman who had once filed a restraining order against an overzealous suitor. He talked to her for over an hour, then met with another woman who had dated the same man. A pattern of behavior began to emerge that he didn't find at all reassuring.

On the flight back to Seattle, Pierce tried to concentrate on the *Times,* but he couldn't relax. Instead, he pulled out his notebook and allowed his thoughts to turn back to Georgia's stalker.

He was well aware that the link between what had happened in Denver and what was happening to Georgia right now was tenuous at best. He certainly had no proof that they could be in any way connected.

He needed more time, more resources, more facts. But with only three more roses to go…

Pierce scanned his list of most likely suspects. His criteria for drawing up this list had been simple. Someone male. Someone with access to the KXPG building. Someone Georgia knew or had met personally, at least once.

Larry Sizemore, the producer who resented Georgia? Mark Evans, the man who'd offered the job that had brought her to Seattle in the first place? Monty Greenfield, the security guard who adored her?

Those were his top three, though it was possible he should add Jack to this list, too. Jack's instability was a problem. And though it sounded like he was just a kid, he could have connections to KXPG that they didn't know about. Like a parent who worked in the building.

Once his plane had landed and the passengers were deboarded, Pierce made his way to the airport parking lot where he'd left his car. He decided to drive straight to Georgia's. It was late, already after eight, and he found himself hoping that she'd given up on him and their plans to have dinner together.

That had been a mistake. He had no business elevating their relation beyond what was necessary for her protection. She thought she liked him, but she was just lonely from being in a strange city. And she was frightened by the stalker. Once her life returned to normal, she would want a boyfriend like that fellow she'd had back home. Someone from a nice family who would make a responsible husband and a good father to her children.

The more he thought about it, the more Pierce realized he should cancel their dinner plans. He powered on his phone and tried her number. No answer. He checked his messages next, but found nothing from her.

Odd. Wasn't she expecting him?

He stepped on the gas, ran an amber light, wove between a couple of slow-moving vehicles. Had she given up on him and gone somewhere else? But that didn't seem like Georgia's style.

As he pulled up to her house, he could see that her car was in the driveway and lights shone from almost every window in her house. Likewise, her neighbor, Fred, appeared to be at home. Walking by the old guy's side of the house, Pierce spotted Georgia's profile through the sheer curtains.

She was visiting Fred. That's why she hadn't answered the phone.

He was relieved that she was safe, but that still left the problem of their dinner to be resolved. Rather than face her now, and run the risk of her changing his mind, as he knew she could do, he decided to drive away and phone her with an apology tomorrow. It was rude, of course, but wasn't that the point?

Pierce traced his steps back to his car, but before he had a chance to get inside, Georgia appeared on Fred's porch.

"I thought that was your car. How was Denver?"

She ran lightly down the sidewalk and stopped within reach. Her smile faded as she saw the expression in his eyes. Her forehead creased with worry lines.

"What's wrong?" she asked.

He wanted to kiss her. Her sweet lips were outlined in a faint, glossy pink and she smelled like vanilla— good enough to eat. She had on a pretty top, with a faded pair of jeans and pointy-toed fashion boots.

"Nothing. Denver was interesting. I have some things to talk to you about. How was Seattle?"

"Wet and dreary."

"I keep telling you, you should have stayed in sunny South Dakota."

She cringed at his cool demeanor. "Did I say something to offend you?"

Everything about you offends me, he wanted to say. *The way you trust, the way you care, the way you smile as if you really mean it.* He could hurt this woman so much, without even trying.

"Of course, you didn't. But it's been a long day. Maybe we should save dinner for another night."

She stared at him, then shook her head. "Oh, no you don't. You're not backing out of this now. Just give me a minute."

She ran into to her place, retrieved a jacket from inside, then came running back. "Coffee and a donut. You can spare me that much."

GEORGIA ORDERED the same thing as the first time. Orange juice and a carrot muffin. A wholesome choice for a wholesome girl. Pierce picked out the most sinfully sugarcoated donut and asked for black coffee.

Georgia selected the same table in the back corner. He sat across from her, wondering what he was doing here. When was he finally going to have the courage to do the right thing and leave her alone?

"Tell me about your brother," she said.

"What?" She'd blindsided him with that one. "How do you know about him?"

"Why shouldn't I?"

Richard London. The damn fool had always been one to talk his head off. "I don't talk about my brother. Not to anyone. Not even Cass, when she was alive."

"Doesn't that seem wrong to you? What was his name?"

"Jay. And if I had wanted you to know about him—"

"Of course you didn't want me to know about your brother. You don't want me to know anything about your past, because then I might understand that you are not nearly as hard and uncaring as you try to pretend."

What a laugh. "You have no idea how innocent you are."

"Not too innocent to realize you loved your brother."

Pierce's chest felt suddenly hot, as if he'd spilled his coffee. But looking at the table, he could see himself holding his mug, hand steady.

"Why is it so hard for you to admit that's true?"

"Love." Pierce spat the word out. "What does that mean, and what good does it do anyone? Jay needed to be saved, that's what he needed. He needed a brother who looked after him and made sure he was okay."

"And maybe you needed a brother like that, too. Maybe if you'd had a brother—or a mother or father—looking out for you, you could have been there for Jay."

"It isn't that easy. What about Cass? I didn't save her, either."

"Who said you needed to? Her accident wasn't your fault, Pierce." Her eyes narrowed. "But you know that, don't you? What do you really feel guilty about, Pierce? If it isn't her accident, it has to be something else."

I didn't love her. He lowered his head so she wouldn't see the truth in his eyes. No, he hadn't loved Cass and he hadn't really been sure about that until now. When he compared how he felt about Georgia to how he'd felt about his wife, he could see exactly what had been missing in his marriage.

And if that wasn't something to feel guilty about, then what was?

"Stop psychoanalyzing me, Georgia. I had enough of that from Cass. She always thought she could 'fix' me, but I'm happy enough the way I am."

"Right."

Georgia didn't say anything, just that word. He sat in silence for a while, wondering if she was mad at him. She didn't seem to be. She continued eating her muffin and sipping her juice. A far cry from the meal he knew she deserved.

He drank some coffee. Couldn't taste it. "Any rose deliveries today?"

"No, thank goodness. It was a quiet day." She told him about dropping into the office, about the strange conversation she'd witnessed between Larry and Rachel.

"Well, that's interesting, especially considering what I found out about your producer today in Denver."

"You went there because of me?" She pulled back in indignation, as he'd known she would.

"Never mind about that. Just listen to this. I tracked down a couple of Larry's ex-girlfriends."

"I didn't know Larry used to live in Denver."

"If you'd run a background check on him you would have. Another thing I found interesting…did you know he's in his early forties?"

"He looks younger than that."

"I know. He takes really good care of himself, including booking into a serious health spa every six months to keep his figure and his skin in good condition."

"Really?" Georgia leaned across the table, her earlier irritation forgotten. "What did you find out about his ex-girlfriends?"

"One of them filed a restraining order against him after they stopped dating. The other complained that she had to actually quit her job because he was in her face so much."

"The guy is off his rocker," Georgia said. "Poor Rachel."

"I hate the idea of you working alone with him at night."

"But Rachel's the one he's obsessed with," Georgia pointed out. "Not me."

"In his mind, you're the reason Rachel won't see him anymore," Pierce pointed out. "God, I wish I could put you under full-time surveillance." He'd toyed with the idea on the plane, but it just wasn't feasible.

"No way, Pierce. I won't have it. Anyway, the notes are annoying and scary, too, but he hasn't ever threatened me."

Pierce wasn't much comforted by that fact.

"Sometimes I wish those last three flowers would just come already. Then, when nothing happens, we'd realize this has just been a cruel hoax."

He wished it could end that simply. "Finished your juice?" he asked, ready to leave though he hadn't touched the donut.

"Fine."

As before, she balled up her garbage and placed the glass bottle in the recycling container.

Since it was still too early to take her to work, he drove her home and walked her to the door. Raindrops drummed on the shingled roof above the porch as she pulled out her key.

"You won't let me pay you, so I'm not a client. You've made it clear you're not romantically interested in me, either. So why do you keep hanging around, Pierce?"

"Getting sick of me, are you?"

"You know better than that. You're just avoiding the question."

Because the question was too astute, that's why. Because he didn't know the answer himself.

"Georgia…?"

"Yes?"

The harsh porch light cast a dark shadow over Georgia's face, but he could still see the warm promise in her eyes, the sweet fullness of her lips. Damn it, he'd reached his limit. He just couldn't resist her anymore.

"Who says I'm not romantically interested?" He put a hand behind her head and kissed her.

CHAPTER TWELVE

THEIR FIRST KISS had been according to Georgia's agenda, initiated by her and controlled by her. This time Pierce was in charge.

He backed her into her house, then pushed the door shut with his body, pulling Georgia with him. She let herself be trapped by his arms, breathless as he devoured her lips with his mouth.

She'd sensed this passion in him the first day she'd met him. Seen glimpses of it in the days following. But he'd rejected her so many times now, she'd begun to suspect he didn't find her attractive after all.

Now, finally, she knew that wasn't true. She kissed him back with equal fire, knowing with certainty how she wanted this particular kiss, with this particular man, to end.

But all too quickly he pulled away. Framing her face within his hands, his voice raspy, he asked, "Is this what you want?"

Georgia could tell he was expecting her to say no.

"One more minute of kissing you and I'm going to carry you up to your bedroom," he warned.

"My thoughts exactly," she assured him. She'd been aching for his touch for weeks. Now she had it. His hands—skimming her shoulders, shucking her trench coat, then curving around her waist—gave her nothing but pleasure.

She put a finger to his mouth and traced the outline of his bottom lip. When she was done, he kissed her again, in a deeply possessive way she'd never experienced before.

"Are you sure you don't want to go back to that farmer in South Dakota?"

After this? "Never."

"Ah, Georgia." He smoothed her hair with his hands, even as his body pressed into hers. "You know I can't be domesticated. I'm not going to marry you, be the father of your babies."

He said all this mockingly, but she knew it was to protect himself, not her.

"Don't tell me what I can't have, Pierce. What *can* you give me?"

"This night. This moment."

"Nothing beyond that?"

He nodded solemnly, but she again did not believe him. God help him, Pierce had so much more to offer than that. She closed her eyes, willing him to kiss her again. He did, slowly and deeply. And after a few moments, she felt him lift her off the ground.

"I warned you what would happen."

"Yes, you did." She nuzzled her face between his

shoulder and neck as he carried her up the old wooden stairs to her bedroom.

She saw his gaze sweep her room, and knew he was checking for signs of invasion. There were none. Her comforter was as smooth as she'd left it. No vase sat on the bedside table. Not a rose was in sight.

He lowered her slowly, and though her feet landed on the floor, she still had the sensation of floating on air. Bit by bit he stripped away her clothing. Then his.

She closed her eyes again and savored each touch of his hands. He was gentle, yet obviously in control. The experience felt new to her, completely unlike the times she'd been with Craig.

"What's wrong? You're frowning." Pierce pressed his lips to her forehead.

"I'm just concentrating. I don't want to forget a second of this." She opened her eyes and saw the anxious look on his face. "Don't worry. I heard you. No marriage. No children. Just tonight. Just this."

As he pulled back the covers on her bed, she switched on the portable CD player.

"I remember that music. You played it the night I stayed for dinner. At the time, I thought the beat was very erotic."

She rotated her hips rhythmically for a few beats. "And what do you think now?"

His gaze locked on the movements of her body, he groaned. "That you always pick the perfect music."

LATER, still holding Georgia in his arms, Pierce's mood had shifted into something relaxed and mellow. After they'd made love, he and Georgia had talked for a while. Now they were just listening to the music. A new song started and he felt an immediate response.

"I've heard her before. What's her name?"

"Bonnie Raitt. 'I Can't Make You Love Me.' Beautiful vocals—and hear that piano? That's Bruce Hornsby, one of my all-time favorite musicians. Bonnie won Grammys with this recording as well."

Though she worked in the music industry, Pierce was still impressed with the way Georgia could rattle off a litany of facts about almost every song she heard. Though in this case, he wondered if she was talking fast in order to mask the poignancy of these particular lyrics.

I can't make you love me. Even he could figure out what Raitt was singing about. Having a man's body but not his heart. Holding him in her arms, even while she knew she could never keep him.

Pierce wrapped his arms tighter around Georgia and closed his eyes. Though the song was saying exactly what he'd told Georgia earlier, he realized he didn't want any of it to be true.

He didn't want to let Georgia go.

She'd seduced him on the radio, but in person her magic was even stronger. This was love. He'd finally found it.

This should have been a very happy moment. But

precisely because he did love her, he knew he couldn't stay with Georgia. He'd been a failure as a husband once. He couldn't put Georgia through that same experience. He could not ruin another person's life.

EVEN THOUGH Pierce's close embrace told her that his emotions were stronger than he was willing to admit, Georgia woke from her brief nap with tears in her eyes.

Feeling uncharacteristically pessimistic, she eased out of the bed and wrapped herself in her robe. What was wrong? Why did she feel so…ominous?

She glanced back at Pierce, sleeping on his side, one arm still curled as if holding her in his dreams. She didn't regret making love with him. That wasn't what this mood was about.

Going to the window, she pulled up the blind. It was raining. She was reminded of the song she'd played for Jack that compared endless rain to the tears from a star.

Jack.

Her stalker?

Or an innocent, troubled boy?

She let go of the blind and went downstairs to put on the CD she'd been thinking of. Sting's music always drove to the center of her heart, and tonight, especially, his music meshed perfectly with the way she was feeling.

This weather, that was the problem. Also the

stalker. Three more roses to go…and then what? She was becoming increasingly tense as she anticipated the final delivery. They could come all at once. Or singly, drawing out the suspense. She didn't know which would be worse.

Cooking was an activity she'd always found comforting and now she took refuge in her kitchen. She scrambled some eggs and made toast. Pierce came down at just the right moment.

Though he greeted her with a smile and a kiss, in his eyes she saw the same unease that she was feeling. The problem wasn't with the two of them, she didn't think. She saw his gaze shift to the control box for her security system and the row of reassuring green lights. *He's worried, too*.

Pierce took glasses from the cupboard and poured them both juice. She brought their full plates to the table. For a few moments they ate in silence.

"Pierce, how much younger was your brother?"

He paused for only a second before answering. "About four years."

"And how old was he when he died?"

"Eleven."

"Tell me what happened."

She'd eased into the topic like wading into a lake, and somehow that approach seemed to work. Pierce sighed, but he didn't get defensive as usual. Stretching out his legs under the table, he started to talk.

"Jay used to skip school a lot. So did I, but I found

it easy enough to catch up on the days I did bother to attend. Jay didn't. His teachers advanced him just to get him out of their classroom."

Georgia nodded. It was a pretty predictable pattern, once started.

"Jay was pretty disruptive. Not mean, but he couldn't keep quiet, couldn't concentrate on any one subject for more than a few minutes. Looking back, I think he probably suffered from fetal alcohol syndrome, which wouldn't be a surprise. Considering how much our mother drank, I can't believe I turned out okay—but then, maybe I give myself too much credit."

She knew better than to give him sympathy. "Fishing for compliments, Pierce?"

He grimaced. "Anyway, just to further set the stage for you, our father was gone more than he was around, which was good because he was a mean drunk. Our mother worked odd jobs off and on, but most afternoons when she was home, she'd start drinking just after lunch and keep going for as long as the wine lasted. She wasn't mean when she was drinking, just emotional and weepy. As soon as we were old enough to tie our laces, Jay and I spent as little time at home as possible."

He looked at her, his face set in a matter-of-fact pose that dared her to suggest that this childhood had been anything but normal. She nodded. "Okay, I get the picture."

"Right. So you can probably guess that Jay being out of school on a Tuesday afternoon wasn't all that uncommon. He and his buddies were hanging around the parking lot of a discount mall about a mile from the school. A semi was backing out of a loading dock, when one of Jay's buddies dared him to cross the truck's path on his bike. Jay would have made it, but his front tire slid on a patch of ice and he went flying. The driver didn't even see him."

"Oh, no. Oh, Pierce." What a stupid, senseless way to die. *Like Cassandra.* The similarity struck Georgia hard. No wonder Pierce couldn't get over his wife's death. He'd never gotten over Jay's.

"He didn't die right away. The truck's rear tires crushed his legs. He'd bled to death, though, by the time the ambulance arrived."

So he'd suffered. And Georgia was willing to bet that Pierce had relived those last minutes of his brother's life over and over and over. And suffered an emotional death each time. "Poor Jay." And poor Pierce. "How did you and your mother find out?"

"The cops phoned our house, but our mother was passed out by then and didn't hear the ringing. They sent someone to the house. I was back from school by then, and I ended up being the one—"

Pierce's gaze slid to the view out the back window, and Georgia wondered what he was seeing. Surely not the bare-branched trees of her backyard. She wondered how many fifteen-year-old boys were required to identify the body of their own dead brother.

"You want to know the ironic thing?"

She nodded, not sure this tale could get any worse.

"Jay died a week before Christmas."

Georgia checked the calendar on her fridge. That was exactly what it was today. A week before the twenty-fifth. A week before the anniversary of his wife's traffic accident, too.

No wonder Pierce hated Christmas.

PIERCE DROVE her to work, the last show of the week. He dropped her off right at the door.

"Thanks for the ride." She paused before walking off. He'd promised her nothing. But he cared. She could see it even now, though he wouldn't look at her.

"Do you want to have dinner tomorrow?" She kept her tone light, as if the answer didn't matter.

"I'll probably be working. But I'll be here to pick you up at the end of your show."

Okay. He needed a little space. Time to process what was happening between them. Stifling the urge to reach over and kiss him, she shut the car door. He didn't drive away until she was safely inside.

As she passed through the revolving glass doors, Georgia felt it again, that sense of boding evil. Trying to shake the mood, she approached the security desk with a smile.

"So, Monty, are you ready for Christmas? I just noticed this afternoon there's only a week to go."

"Oh, I don't have much to do to get ready. How about you? Are you going home for the holidays?"

"Because of my show, I've only got the weekend." She hadn't felt right asking for extra days off when she was so new to the job. "I fly out Christmas morning and have to return two days later. It'll be short, but I've never spent a Christmas away from my family."

Then she realized that Monty would be facing his first Christmas without his wife. "I'm sorry, that was thoughtless. This is going to be a tough time for you, isn't it?"

"Since we didn't have kids, we never did fuss much over holidays. What about that new fellow you've been seeing? Taking him home to meet the parents?"

Pierce at her home in South Dakota? Now there was a novel thought. "I think it's a little soon for that."

Monty nodded. "You don't want to rush these things."

Wondering what she could do to make this first Christmas on his own easier for Monty, Georgia rushed up the stairs and almost bumped into Larry as he was leaving her studio.

"Larry?" What had he been doing in her room?

He put a hand to the neat beard at his chin. "Hi,

Georgia. I just wanted to tell you that the Thursday show was really amazing."

The compliment, coming from Larry, was a shock. "Really?"

"Yeah. I guess Mark knew what he was doing putting you in this time slot. I'm sorry I wasn't more welcoming at the beginning."

"Oh."

Larry's milk-chocolate eyes looked at her steadily. He seemed completely sincere.

"I appreciate you saying that. I always did think we could make a great team if we could work together."

Larry nodded. "The sky's the limit. Once we're syndicated, we'll definitely be in the big league."

He knew about the syndication offer? Mark must have spoken to him, too. Suddenly Georgia was very cynical about Larry's change of heart. He'd identified her as a rising star and was determined that his career would advance along with hers.

What a jerk.

"I'd better get some prep work done for my show."

"Sure." He stepped aside so she could get into her studio.

Once inside, she looked around carefully, searching for anything out of place. She didn't like the idea of Larry's snooping around. And she didn't buy his excuse that he'd come in to congratulate her. One glance through the window that divided his control room from her studio would have told him she wasn't there.

So what had he really been doing here?

CHAPTER THIRTEEN

As he'd promised, Pierce was waiting for Georgia after the show. He met her at the door to escort her from the building, looking tired and unshaven and dangerously attractive. Georgia hoped he would reach out and give her a kiss, but all he did was open the car door for her.

"The show was good," he said shortly. "Any problems?"

She waited until he was in the car with her to answer. "Not really. I found Larry in my studio when I arrived, though. I have no idea what he was doing there."

"No roses, I hope?" He started the engine and headed toward her home.

"None. Everything seemed as I left it. Except Larry. Now that there's talk of my show becoming syndicated, all of a sudden he's being all friendly and supportive."

"What a snake," Pierce commented. "Have you heard from Rachel Masterson if he's been bothering her lately?"

"I had an e-mail," Georgia said. "She's dating someone else. She didn't mention Larry at all."

"Maybe the guy is finally developing some maturity. By the way, while you were on the air, I tracked down some interesting information about Monty."

"Monty? You're being very thorough in these background checks of yours. Next thing you're going to tell me you've been investigating Fred."

"As a matter of fact..."

"Really?" She twisted in her seat to see his face. He was serious. He'd really done a background check on Fred.

Why did he insist on suspecting everyone who was closest to her? If they found this stalker—*when* they found him—she wanted it to be a stranger. Preferably someone she'd never even spoken to on the phone before.

They were already in front of her house. Pierce pulled in behind her car. "Let's talk about this inside," he suggested calmly.

But Georgia felt far from calm as she unlocked her front door and entered her security code.

"Would you mind making me a sandwich or something?" Pierce asked. "I'm starving."

She wanted to start ranting at him, right then, right there. But the nurturing instinct was too strong. She made him his sandwich, then vented her frustration by banging the plate on the table when she set it in front of him.

"Pierce, there has to be a limit. You have to trust *some people* in life."

"Why?" He took a bite of the sandwich and nodded his approval. "This is good. I like the avocado."

"Forget the avocado. You have to trust people because otherwise you'd go crazy. Either that, or turn into some sort of machine."

"I pick the machine."

He said that, but she didn't believe him. Couldn't believe him. She sat in the chair opposite his and leaned her arms onto the table.

"For instance," she said, illustrating her point, "I trust you."

Pierce stopped chewing. "You do?"

"Of course I do. I could have been suspicious about you from the start. After all, I met you the night I found the first rose. You were at just the right place at just the right time. Maybe you put it there. Maybe, while you've been pretending to protect me, you've been the one leaving all the flowers and notes."

"How ingeniously clever of me," he murmured.

She slapped his hand lightly. "Don't be an idiot."

He set down his sandwich, suddenly serious. "You raise a good point, though, Georgia. You should be more careful. You *should* be suspicious of me. In fact, why aren't you?"

She rolled her eyes. "You're asking for facts, aren't you? Well, I don't have any of those. I just know. That's all. Just like I know Fred isn't my stalker. Good heavens, he's a lonely old man with a fading memory and bad knees. Can you really imagine Fred sneaking inside the KXPG offices to leave me those roses?"

"He could have hired someone…."

Georgia made a noise of disbelief.

"Okay. I agree that was a long shot. I just wanted to ensure that he really has lived in this neighborhood as long as he says he has."

"And…?"

"He's owned his house since 1964."

"Of course he has. So we agree Fred's off the list of suspects?"

Pierce nodded. "Now let's talk about Monty."

Georgia's first instincts were to leap to his defense, too. After all, in the beginning he'd been one of her few friends at KXPG. But she really didn't know him that well. Not as well as she knew Fred.

"Okay, I'll bite. What did you find out about Monty?"

"Did you know he has his bachelor of science in pharmacy?"

"Yes, isn't it amazing? He told me he got tired of working with old, sick people. And being on his feet all day."

"I can see that. But why decide to be a security guard?"

"He said his father was one." She shrugged. "Also,

he wanted to work around young people. And there's lots of young people in the communications business. Was that all you found out about him? That he has a university education?"

"Did you know the wife that just passed away was his second?"

"I didn't. What happened to his first wife?"

"Wife number one had diabetes. She died of hypoglycemia, which is a deficiency of blood sugar caused by an overdose of insulin. His second wife had asthma. She died of respiratory failure."

"Maybe that's another reason he didn't want to be around sick people anymore." Having watched both of his wives suffer that way... "Poor Monty."

"Or smart Monty. Maybe he married sick women, hoping they would die."

"Lord, you are cynical, aren't you?" She eyed him suspiciously. "There's something else, isn't there? Who else did you check into?"

"Your program director," he admitted.

"Mark? He's the nicest guy. And he has kids!"

Pierce quelled her objections with a dark look.

"Okay, I know lots of criminals seem like nice guys to their neighbors and co-workers and even their children. But it's in Mark's best interest for my show to do well. After all, he's the one who discovered me and hired me. Why would he sabotage all that effort by sending me roses and trying to scare me?"

"Mark Evans isn't only a program director. He's

a man who was deserted by his wife. You don't know how he feels about that deep inside. He could be resentful, angry, frustrated…."

"Maybe." Well, he'd be less than human if he didn't feel at least some of what Pierce described. "But why take out his negative emotions on me?"

"Cass used to talk about this thing called *transference*."

She shook her head. "Okay, fine, I guess it's a theory, but it doesn't sit right with me."

"In this case, your instincts are probably on target. Mark Evans checks out to be exactly what he seems to be—a solid family man whose world was rocked when his wife left him to further her career. He has a nice steady employment record, a solid financial history and no criminal record."

"See? I told you."

"Georgia, none of that proves he isn't our guy. It just makes it less likely."

She went to the fridge to pour herself some juice. "So where does all this get us? Do you really think any of these men could be my stalker?"

"If I had to put my money on someone right this minute—" Pierce paused, then finally decided "—it would have to be Larry. Maybe he thinks if he scares you badly enough, you'll go back to South Dakota and Rachel will get her job back."

"Hmm. I guess that isn't the dumbest theory I've ever heard."

"I went to the apartment building where he lives last night and talked to some of his neighbors. Apparently he hasn't dated anyone since Rachel. So he's probably still hung up on her."

"Oh, dear, you may be right about Larry. He's being so nice all of a sudden, but that could be a ploy. He isn't a stupid man. He's got to know we'd be suspicious of him."

"What I hate is knowing you spend every night working with the creep."

"I just have to hit one button and Monty will be right there," she assured him. She leaned farther over the table and covered her head with her arms. "I really, really hate this. It's bad enough that someone I work with might be responsible for this awful mess.

"But what if it isn't Larry? What if it isn't any of the people you think it might be? The stalker could be anyone in Seattle who's listened to my show."

"Even me."

She shot him an annoyed look. "Would you shut up about that already?"

He chuckled. "Shut up? Watch your language, lady." He swallowed the last of his sandwich, then pushed himself out of his chair. "I'd better be leaving."

She thought of how empty and quiet her house was going to feel when he was gone. Not to mention her bed. "Are you sure?"

"Absolutely."

He met her gaze squarely, and she didn't miss the message. He may have slept with her once, but he didn't intend for it to happen again.

She walked him to the entry and opened the door. He glanced up to the hidden camera in the porch roof. "You'll let me know if…anything happens?"

"Yes." She almost wished something would happen, that her stalker would leave another rose on the porch. All she wanted was for this to be over so she could concentrate on what really mattered to her. Her relationship with Pierce.

SINCE PIERCE had made it clear he had no intention of spending any portion of the weekend with her, Georgia decided to call Rachel to see if she was free for dinner.

"I'm glad you phoned. I'm at loose ends and I hate not having plans on a Saturday night."

Just hearing the other woman's voice lightened Georgia's mood. "What about the new guy you've been seeing?"

"He had to go out of town. To Mexico."

"Well, we could pretend we're in Mexico," Georgia improvised. "Do you know any good Mexican restaurants?"

She carried the portable phone up the stairs to the bathroom and opened the cabinet door where she kept her makeup.

"You bet I do. Say, why are *you* free tonight? I

hear there's a dark, mysterious hunk who's been escorting you back and forth from the station every night."

"I'd be very interested to find out exactly what you've heard. And from whom."

"Ah, that would be telling," Rachel teased.

They made plans to meet in an hour at the restaurant. Georgia put on a little mascara and eyeliner, then a fresh coat of lipstick. She changed into a pair of black slacks and a sexy red sweater. It was almost Christmas after all.

Her heart raced as she ran from her house to her car, but she didn't spot any roses on the porch or on her windshield, or any of the other places she'd been afraid she might find one. On the drive to the restaurant, she kept checking her rearview mirror anxiously, in case she was being followed.

She spotted nothing suspicious.

In the restaurant, with Rachel, she finally relaxed. They ordered margaritas and nachos and bowls of thick and spicy black bean soup. As before, Georgia felt immediately at ease in the other woman's company.

"So how are things going with Larry?" Rachel asked, nibbling on a salsa-loaded tortilla chip.

"He's done a complete about-face." Georgia told her about his compliment as well as the possibility of syndication.

"Well, that explains it. He's hitching his star to

your wagon, my dear. Don't be too surprised if his next step is to ask you out."

"Oh. Surely not."

"I wouldn't put it past him."

"But he still likes you." Georgia confessed to having overheard their conversation in the supply room.

"Larry's pride was hurt, that's all. He doesn't really care about me."

"He isn't…bothering you excessively, is he?" Pierce's information about Larry's ex-girlfriends had Georgia concerned on Rachel's behalf as well as her own.

"He was a nuisance for a while. But last time I caught him skulking around my apartment building, I came out ready to fight. He didn't expect that from a woman." Rachel winked. "Thing is, I'm more than capable of giving that twerp a black eye. And he knows it, too."

"I'm glad you have the situation under control." She remembered the other bit of interesting information Pierce had told her. "By the way, did you know Nancy was Monty's second wife?"

Rachel looked surprised. "Really? I thought they'd been married forever. But I guess I just assumed."

An electronic melody sounded, and Rachel pulled out her cell phone. "Sorry, I forgot to turn this off." She checked the number before tucking it back into her purse.

"If you want to take the call, go ahead."

Rachel shook her head. "Nope. I'll just let him wonder what I'm up to for a while."

Georgia laughed. "Tell me about him. Where did you meet?"

"At a charity thing I was doing for the station. But first you tell me about that arresting new man in your life. He looks like he might be undercover FBI or something. Dangerous, but yummy, too."

Georgia smiled, understanding exactly what Rachel meant. "Actually he's a private investigator who used to be a cop with the Seattle Police Department. We're not really dating, though I wish we were, to be honest. He's been helping me with a little problem."

"Is this about the roses?"

She should have known Rachel would have heard.

"Monty and Mark both told me you have a so-called secret admirer. What a pain for you, but that's one of the hazards of our business. I remember a few years ago I made the mistake of saying I liked a certain brand of chocolate. For weeks later, this strange man kept sending me deliveries of the stuff. Both to work and to my home address, which frankly, I found a little eerie."

"I know exactly how you feel." Did she ever. It was so wonderful to talk to someone who had been through this, too. Maybe the roses weren't such a big deal, after all.

"Finally I called the police and they tracked the

guy down through the courier company. He'd paid with his Visa, the poor fool. His wife was not happy when she found out what he'd been up to. He never sent me another chocolate after that!"

Georgia was relieved to hear the story had such an innocuous ending. "Did he send you any notes with the chocolates?"

"Sure. Silly things like, 'I love you. You're the best.' The sort of messages you'd get on those candy Valentine hearts."

Georgia's heart sank. Rachel's notes didn't sound anything like hers.

"You've had notes too?" Rachel guessed.

Georgia nodded. "He claims that after he's given me a dozen roses, I'll be his. So far I've received nine. Three to go."

"That's creepy." Rachel put her hand over Georgia's. "Have you called the police?"

"Yes, but unfortunately they don't have much to go on. He's never had the roses delivered to the same place twice and so we haven't been able to catch him in the act."

"The jerk. He probably has no idea how much he's frightening you."

Georgia didn't say anything, but in her heart she disagreed. Her stalker knew he was scaring her. In fact, he wanted to scare her.

CHAPTER FOURTEEN

THE CHURCH SERVICE that Reid's wife, Moira, favored was on Sunday morning at eleven o'clock. Sylvie knew this because most weeks Reid would meet her at that time, stealing in with take-out lattes and the weekend paper. On those mornings, they didn't sleep together, and Sylvie had always found them sweet.

This week, though, when Reid asked if he could come over with coffee and bagels, she said no. She was wearing his ring when she made this decision. Staring down at her beautiful new artificial nails and the dazzling diamond on her fourth finger, she almost didn't recognize her own hand.

"Not this time, Reid. I have something else planned."

She could tell he wasn't pleased, but he didn't press her any further.

"Oh. Okay."

She hung up the phone, then went to her closet. She chose a simple black skirt with a turtleneck and a tweed jacket. She would have to carry an umbrella because it was raining again.

She asked the cab driver to let her off a block from the Madison Park United Church. Though it was only ten-thirty, worshipers were already gathering. Of course, with Christmas only a week away, crowds would be larger than usual.

Or so Sylvie supposed. She hadn't been to church for years, except for the odd wedding. Wayne's family hadn't been religious at all, nor had her mother been one for regular church attendance. She'd been big on spending Sunday with her daughter, though. Sylvie remembered well their afternoon jaunts—usually to the museum or art gallery, but occasionally something lighter like a movie.

Sylvie tied a knot into the scarf she'd wrapped around her neck, then set out determinedly for the church. Rain rapped lightly against her umbrella and water seeped through the fine leather of her shoes, making her feet cold and damp.

Once inside, she selected a pew near the back, then sat, waiting.

Fifteen minutes later, a woman in her late thirties or early forties walked in alone. She had on a trench coat and kept her head bowed as she walked up the aisle. Sylvie couldn't say how she knew this woman was Reid's wife, but she did. She craned her neck for a better view of the other woman, but only managed a quick glimpse of her profile before she settled in a pew on the other side of the center aisle.

Now all Sylvie could see was the back of the woman's head—brunette hair against the lighter brown of her coat. Sylvie remembered once pulling a long dark hair from the back of Reid's wool jacket.

Apparently he did not go through the same ritual of cleaning himself before coming to see her as the other way around.

Music played, the choir sang, then the minister spoke and made announcements. Sylvie didn't absorb a single word of the service. All her attention was focused on that one particular woman.

Where were the kids? Sunday school? A baby-sitter? When Moira bent her head to pray, Sylvie wondered what it was she was asking for. Did she know her husband was thinking of leaving her? That he was in love with someone else?

Sylvie kept very still not wishing to draw anyone's attention. But, she found herself wishing that just once Moira would turn and look at her.

That didn't happen, though, until after the service, when the worshippers were filing out through the center aisle. The ushers called on the front rows first, and after about five minutes, Moira rose to her feet and joined the procession. As she neared the rear of the church, her gaze traveled down Sylvie's row. For a second their eyes met.

Sylvie held her breath, wondering, *Does she know me? Is it possible?*

But no flash of recognition registered on the other

woman's face. Moira looked pretty, but visibly tired and...sad?

Sylvie dropped her gaze to her lap, where her hands were twisted so tightly together she couldn't even see the ring she still wore.

"LOOK OUTSIDE, Seattle. The sun is shining today so make sure you take advantage of the break in our weather," the male announcer said. "Tomorrow the rain will be back, with a possibility of snow later in the week. Could it be we'll have a white Christmas after all?"

Pierce groaned, then rolled over in his bed. The radio had been playing for half an hour, though he'd done his best to ignore it. Now, predictably, the oh-so-familiar strains of "Let It Snow! Let It Snow! Let It Snow!" defiled the solitude of his bedroom.

He groaned again, then rolled out of bed, noting that it was almost noon. Though he'd been in bed for almost six hours, he felt as if he'd barely slept a wink. Obviously his body clock was skewed from all those late nights of listening to *Seattle after Midnight.*

Leaving the radio blaring, he headed to the ensuite bathroom where he turned on the shower, then brushed his teeth as he waited for the water to get hot. Standing in front of the mirror, he rubbed a hand over the stubble on his chin. From the open door to his bedroom, he could hear the stupid Christmas song end, and the news announcer come on.

He leaned closer to the mirror. Tiny red lines spiraled out from his pupils like little spiderwebs. *God, you're a mess.*

His head pounded as if he had a hangover, though he hadn't had any alcohol to drink since the last time he'd shared a bottle of wine with Georgia. He stepped into the shower and hoped the fresh, warm water would clear his brain.

Instead, he found himself tormented by the same song that had been repeating itself in his mind last night as he tossed from one side to the other in a vain attempt to sleep.

Georgia had played the song on her Friday show and somehow it had resonated with him. It was a Blue Rodeo tune where a guy admits to his lover, that, yes, he's made mistakes, but he isn't bulletproof, either. He suffers, too, though he might not show it.

Scenes from his marriage to Cass played through his head at the same time, much as they'd done last night. It was as if that song were the title track to a movie and the movie was his life.

Get a grip, Harding. What do you think you are—a poet?

He was the furthest thing possible from that. He was a cop turned investigator, a man trained to deal with facts. And these were the facts concerning his own life these days.

He was losing his appetite. His nights were becoming increasingly restless, disturbed by dreams from his past, as well as an aching yearning for a woman and a future that were beyond his grasp. Meanwhile, his employees were holding his business together while he spent more and more time trying to figure out who the hell was stalking Georgia—and why.

The why was important, because that would tell him whether the roses and the notes were just nuisances…or if they represented a physical threat and real danger.

Increasingly he was fearful of the latter. And he suspected Georgia, despite the cheerful perspective she had on life, was feeling the same sense of looming menace.

He had to figure out what was happening. And soon.

In his mind he mapped out his plans for the day. Maybe he'd been too quick to dismiss Jack from his list of suspects. Was there any way he could try to track the kid down? Georgia had told him his number came up as unlisted whenever he dialed the station. Were there any other clues he'd missed?

Also, he needed to follow up with Monty's stepdaughter from his first marriage. According to his research, she lived here in Seattle. He wondered if there was bad blood between them since Georgia had mentioned several times that Monty would be spending Christmas alone.

That might be interesting to check out, too.

Pierce's plans for the day were forgotten the moment he turned off the water. In the sudden quiet, he could hear the radio announcer's voice clearly.

"...our own Georgia from *Seattle after Midnight* will be wrapping gifts from one o'clock until five. So make sure you head down to Bellevue Square today to finish up that last-minute shopping. All proceeds will benefit the food bank during this holiday season...."

Dripping wet, Pierce walked out to his bedroom where he stared at the clock radio in helpless fury.

Surely this couldn't be right? Georgia couldn't be this foolish...could she? Not only going out into a public mall where anyone would have access to her...but having her presence there announced to the entire city on top of it all?

Even as he prayed this was all a big mistake, Pierce knew it wasn't. *Damn it, she was a crazy woman.* Why hadn't she at least told him about this?

"I'M SO EXCITED to meet you. In person!" The elderly woman beamed at Georgia. "My insomnia is so bad, some nights I sleep only three or four hours. Your show is a real godsend."

"That's sweet of you to say." Georgia folded over the edge of the foil paper, then secured it with a length of tape. She flipped the box over and added the final touch—a garland of ribbon with a miniature candy cane attached.

"I hope your grandniece gets a lot of wear out of her sweater." She handed over the gaily wrapped parcel, with a pang of compassion for this sweet old lady. She'd probably done her best to select a gift her thirteen-year-old niece would enjoy, but Georgia suspected this box would be coming back to the mall the week after Christmas.

"Thank you, dear. And if you could remember about the Sinatra…"

"I will do my best," Georgia promised. "Merry Christmas, Mrs. Corbis."

"Merry Christmas to you, too, dear."

Georgia circled her shoulders in an attempt to ease the stiffness as the next person in the long line of shoppers waiting for gift wrapping stepped up to her table. She'd been here for three hours now…just one more to go.

"Hi, I'm Georgia." She held out her hand to the tall gawky boy in front of her. He'd already paid his five dollars to Cindy, the volunteer from the food bank working the kiosk with Georgia today.

"I'm Brady Walsh." His poor, acne-marked face turned a brilliant red as he dumped a bag onto the table. "Could you wrap this for my Mom? It's just a book."

"My favorite kind of present," she said, trying to put him at ease. She slipped the volume out of the bag, then nodded approvingly. "I've read this. Great choice. Now would you like the red foil or the white paper with the holly pattern?"

"You pick."

"The holly pattern. It's the more sophisticated of the two, I think." She rolled out a portion of the paper, measuring the length with an experienced eye. As she cut, she asked, "My radio show is probably too late for you. Have you ever heard it?"

"I listen all the time," he assured her.

She smiled, hearing the enthusiasm of a true fan in his voice. "But you must be tired at school the next day?"

"I catch up with my sleep on the weekends."

As Georgia folded neat corners in the paper, she automatically glanced into the throng around her. The mall had been packed since she arrived, which should have made her less nervous. If she wasn't safe in a crowd this size, where could she feel safe?

And yet all afternoon she'd had the eerie sensation of being watched. She checked out the coffee bar across from her kiosk. In the back, a man was sitting reading the paper. He'd been there for over an hour. He had on a ball cap and was mostly hidden by a rack of travel mugs, so she'd only caught a few glimpses of him.

No need to worry. Even if he is the stalker, what can he do to me here?

She finished wrapping the book and attached the final decorative bow. "Here you go, Brady. I'm sure your mom will appreciate her terrific son on Christmas morning."

He blushed again, then turned to leave.

Georgia smiled at the next shopper as he stepped forward, this one a man in his forties. He carried a bag from a popular lingerie shop.

Red foil, she decided, even as she'd begun her introduction. "Hi, I'm Georgia."

"Good to meet you, Georgia. My wife and I love your show. I'm Rick by the way. Could you wrap this for my wife? I'm a real klutz when it comes to jobs like this."

"Sure, I'll do it up real pretty for you." Without looking she reached for the paper, then winced as something pricked her hand. "Ouch!"

She turned to see what had happened. Two roses lay on the table next to the rolls of wrapping paper. *Oh, Lord. Oh, no.* Two more roses.

Her heart thudded as she ripped the note from the stems and shoved it into her purse.

"Who put these here?" She pointed out the blossoms to Cindy.

"I didn't see anything." The woman shrugged.

"I guess you have a secret admirer," Rick teased, not guessing how much fear his words brought to her.

Instinctively, Georgia glanced back at the coffee shop. The man with the newspaper had disappeared.

PIERCE, PRETENDING to examine the selection of CDs at the front rack of a music store, saw Georgia's face turn white. A moment later she lifted two crimson roses from her table.

Hell. Where had those come from?

He stopped thumbing through the CDs and quickly exited the store. Dodging the mass of Christmas shoppers, he wove his way to the gift-wrapping kiosk, past the long line of waiting patrons.

"Are you okay?" he called to Georgia, as soon as he was near enough for her to hear.

She dropped the roses to the floor. "I'm fine. What are you doing here?"

Her gaze shot to the coffee shop across the wide hall. Had she seen someone there?

"I was Christmas shopping," he lied. He scooped the roses from the floor. "Did you see anything?"

"No. One minute the flowers weren't here. The next they were. I did think there was someone watching me in that coffee shop earlier," she pointed, "but he's gone now."

"I can't believe I didn't see him." Pierce scanned the crowd, examining faces suspiciously. Whoever had delivered these flowers couldn't have gone far. The volume of people made it impossible to walk quickly, let alone run.

But the stalker, whoever he was, blended in perfectly.

Where are you, you bastard?

"Was there a note?" he asked Georgia, not taking

his eye off the hordes. God, he hated this holiday. Look at all these people, caught up in the mistaken belief that life would be wonderful if they could just find the perfect Christmas gift.

"Yes. It's in my purse. We'll have to look at it later. I'm supposed to be wrapping Christmas gifts for another forty minutes."

She attached a fussy ribbon and candy cane to the top of the present she'd just finished wrapping and handed it to the man at the front of the line.

"Here you go, Rick. Thank you for being so patient. And Merry Christmas."

Pierce found himself resenting the smile she gave to the man, and the admiring glance that he gave her in exchange. An older gentleman moved forward next. Georgia introduced herself, then started to measure out wrapping paper with shaking hands.

"Let me help you." Pierce put his hand over hers.

"Are you sure?"

He nodded, then began to roll out the paper. For Cass's birthday and Valentine's Day gifts he'd always relied on helpful store clerks. As a result, he'd never wrapped a present before in his life.

But how hard could it be?

FOR THE NEXT forty minutes Georgia forgot to worry about her stalker as she enjoyed the spectacle of watching Pierce learn to wrap Christmas gifts.

"Let me handle that for you, ma'am," he said to

one woman, about his age. He measured out foil paper for the large box.

"I listen to your show all the time when I'm working nights at the hospital," the woman told Georgia. Then she looked at Pierce. "But who are you?"

"Hired help," Georgia said. "But he needs training." She watched as Pierce mangled a corner, then tried to compensate for his mistake with too much tape.

The woman laughed. "You remind me of my husband."

"Is he drop-dead gorgeous, too?" Pierce asked.

"Idiot," Georgia said, to keep from laughing. She snatched the parcel from him and her hands quickly became steady again as she smoothed out his mistakes. "Fold the corners like this—see? Just like making a bed."

"I prefer messing the bed." Pierce handed her a piece of tape. "But that's just me."

The last hour passed more quickly than the previous three all together. Soon Cindy was packing up the remaining gift-wrapping paper and thanking Georgia for her time.

"We made a pile of money. The society is going to be so grateful."

"It was a pleasure to help," Georgia said, meaning it. She enjoyed the opportunity to meet her listeners and she'd definitely seen another side of Pierce when he'd stepped in to help her.

"Did you drive here?" Pierce asked her.

"Yes."

"I'll walk you to your car."

They said goodbye to Cindy, then prepared to leave.

"Oh, wait," Cindy called. She picked up the two roses from the floor. "Don't forget your flowers."

IN THE END, Pierce opted to ride home with Georgia.

"I'll pick up my car later. We have some things we need to discuss."

Georgia felt like rolling her eyes. She could well imagine what he meant.

They found her bright-yellow car in the jammed parking lot and Pierce folded his long frame into the passenger seat. Georgia had no sooner backed out of her space than he started on her.

"Can you explain why you didn't tell me you were doing this gift-wrapping thing?"

Georgia wasn't sure whether to give him an honest answer. She was hurt that he hadn't wanted anything to do with her this weekend. And she was tired of using her stalker as an excuse to get his attention.

"I didn't tell you, because I knew you'd feel obligated to come keep an eye on me." She shot him a pointed glance. "Which you did anyway."

"After I heard the announcement on the radio. And, yeah, I beat it right over here. Come on, Georgia. Even you must see that wrapping gifts in an overcrowded shopping mall was an unnecessary risk. Why didn't you tell your boss you couldn't do it?"

"Christmas is a busy time of year for us. The requests from local charities are overwhelming. I'm part of the team at KXPG and I need to do my share."

"Under the circumstances, everyone would have understood if you'd chosen to bow out of this one."

"Maybe," she conceded. "But I'm finished now, so let's not argue about it anymore."

Pierce picked up the roses she'd thrown on the dash. "The guy has nerve. He must have been just a couple of feet away from you when he dropped these on the table."

"I could have seen him—heck, I could have wrapped a Christmas gift for him—and not realized who he was."

Pierce said nothing to that. It was a sobering thought.

GEORGIA DROVE into the parking lane on her side of the duplex. She removed the keys from the ignition, then turned to Pierce.

"Want to come in?" She gathered her purse and the roses from the car.

He nodded. "I'll need to call a cab." He wouldn't stay any longer than necessary. It wouldn't be safe. The urge to hold Georgia was getting stronger by the moment. He couldn't give in to such a dangerous impulse. Not again.

As they walked to the door, Pierce observed Fred standing by his window. Georgia waved and Fred waved back.

"He's such a good neighbor," Georgia commented as she unlocked the door.

Pierce noticed that the act of punching in her security code was now second nature to her.

For a moment they stood in the hall awkwardly. Not looking at each other, but not knowing where else to look.

"I'd better call that cab." He reached into his pocket for his cell phone and dialed the company he usually used.

"They'll have someone here in fifteen minutes."

"Might as well come in, then." Georgia took his jacket and hung it on the newel post on the stairs. Then she went to the kitchen. He followed her there. She still had the roses in her hand. Now she stuffed them into the kitchen trash.

"Want anything to eat? I have some stew I could heat up in five minutes in the microwave."

Georgia was always offering him food. "No thanks. I'd like to look at that note, though."

Her face fell. "I'd forgotten about that." She went to retrieve it from her purse.

Like the others, this one had been wrapped around the stems of the roses and was punctured in several places from the thorns. Nevertheless, the short message was easy to read.

On the first day of Christmas my true love gave to me...one perfect red rose. Just one more to come, Georgia. Then you'll be mine forever.

CHAPTER FIFTEEN

FOR THE FIVE DAYS leading up to Christmas Eve, Pierce drove Georgia to and from all her shows. Terrified of finding that last rose, Georgia stuck close to home when she wasn't at work. She busied herself with Christmas baking, putting together gift baskets of shortbread and gingersnaps for Fred, Monty, Rachel, Mark Evans and his kids, and even Larry.

But as she mixed dough and transferred cookie sheets back and forth from the oven, she wasn't thinking of any of these people.

Pierce. The man was showing up on her doorstep every day like a faithful chauffeur, but she saw no glimpse of the lover she'd known so briefly. When he'd promised her just the one night, he'd been more serious than she could have ever guessed.

He had to feel the same void, the same aching need that she did. But she was losing confidence that he would ever give in to the desires of his heart. He escorted her to and from work in such determined silence. She didn't know if he even listened to her show anymore.

She would have been angry if it wasn't so clear that he was suffering. She could tell he wasn't getting much sleep, and she guessed he was losing weight, too.

Was it the approaching holiday that had him so stressed? His brother had died the week before Christmas. His wife fatally injured on Christmas Eve. In his past did Pierce have even one happy Christmas to remember?

Probably not.

Whereas she had nothing but joyful memories of family dinners, gift exchanges by the tree, then evenings spent playing charades and Name That Tune.

They were so different. That she felt this connection to him was strange. And yet, even if he disappeared from her life tomorrow, she knew she would never forget him. Never feel this same sense of belonging with another man.

She couldn't give up on him. If waiting patiently wasn't going to work, she had to try something else. But was there any way of breaking down his barriers after all he'd been through?

"GOOD EVENING, Seattle, and welcome to our Christmas Eve show." Georgia had her mouth right next to the mike. On her desk, by her right hand, sat a huge, insulated mug of hot chocolate…compliments of Larry.

"Merry Christmas," he'd said as he'd handed her

the festive new insulated mug filled with her favorite hot beverage.

She'd been doubly glad, then, that she'd brought in a basket of her baking for him. She had one for her family, too, which she'd packed in a duffel bag along with her other presents.

She'd distributed all her other baking earlier, except for Pierce's, which she'd left on the kitchen table at home. In the end she'd been too angry with him to give him the gift. He'd been so stubborn and cool all week long. She'd had enough of him and his attitude.

She'd even turned down his offer to drive her to the airport after her show to catch the six-forty-five flight to Sioux Falls. "I'll take a cab," she'd said, and he'd just shrugged. As if he didn't care what she did.

And maybe he didn't. Maybe she'd been wrong about him all along. Maybe when he'd said he wasn't capable of loving, he was right. At least where she was concerned.

She closed her mind on that depressing conclusion and injected brightness into her voice as she leaned into the mike.

"In theory, since it's after midnight, this is Christmas Day. But we're going to ignore technicalities tonight and linger in Christmas Eve land for the next five hours. I have a mix of seasonal music and my own favorite tunes that I hope will put you in the perfect holiday mood."

With that she turned off her mike and queued up Jewel's "Joy to the World." Leaning back in her chair, she took a sip of the hot chocolate as she scanned that evening's play list. The next song was by the Dixie Chicks. Reading the title gave her an idea.

Yes. That was exactly what tonight's show should be about.

When the traditional Christmas carol she'd chosen for her opening number ended, she had the pretty ballad queued up and ready.

"Tonight millions of children are being asked if they believe in Santa Claus. I have a different question for you, Seattle. Do you believe in love? Let's ask three chicks from Austin, Texas, what they think…."

FROM HER DARKENED living room, Sylvie saw a pair of headlights creep up her street. On *Seattle after Midnight,* the Dixie Chicks were singing "I Believe in Love." As usual, Georgia's show had her thinking. Did she believe in love?

And was what she and Reid shared together really love? Or just a desire, on both their parts, to escape from everyday reality? Reid had been married many years. He had children and responsibilities, and maybe he hungered for the days of his youth.

As for her, she'd longed to escape the black period of her life that had begun with her mother's death. Her affair with Reid had provided the perfect diversion.

The car outside pulled into her driveway. Reid had already told her he couldn't spend the holiday with his family and pretend nothing was wrong. So had he asked for a divorce? Was he coming to her now—a free man at last?

The headlights on the car went out. Shortly after, she heard a tapping at her door. She pulled her robe tight and after checking the peephole, let in her guest.

Reid stepped inside. He looked at her without saying a word, his entire being radiating anxiety, need, guilt.

"Are you okay?" she asked.

They still hadn't touched each other. Usually they embraced the second Reid was in the door.

But tonight, Sylvie felt as if a physical force were somehow holding them apart. Reid, in his trench coat and wool trousers—probably the outfit he'd worn earlier to church—stood on the mat, hands clenched around his car keys.

Sylvie pulled her velour robe even tighter. She saw Reid's gaze drop to her hands.

"You aren't wearing your ring."

"No." She'd taken it off after the church service and hadn't put it on since. She hadn't told him that she'd staked out his wife's church the previous Sunday. With all the extra holiday commitments that went along with this time of year, they'd been unable to see each other for almost a week. She looked at Reid, looked deeply into his eyes.

"It's over, isn't it?" she said.

He exhaled a heavy breath filled with sorrow. "It hurts to say this, but I think you're right. I love you, Sylvie, but breaking up a family…my family…is harder than I ever thought."

"I know." Seeing Moira last Sunday had made Reid's wife and kids real to her for the very first time. After the service she'd seen the woman collect two pink-cheeked children from their Sunday school classes. She'd realized then that what was happening here could never be right.

"After that last night we spent together I went home planning to tell Moira and get it over with. But I couldn't. I just couldn't."

He put a hand to his face, struggling to regain control. And though her instinct was to comfort him, Sylvie remained standing where she was.

"I didn't want to face my family on Christmas morning knowing I was a liar and a cheat. I want to set things right with my wife. This is the last time I can ever talk to you."

A part of her felt like cheering, even though she mostly felt overwhelmingly sad. No point in telling Reid that she, herself, had come to the same conclusion.

"Let me get the ring." She started to turn, but Reid stopped her with his hand on her arm.

"I don't want it back. I don't care what you do with it. Sell it in the classifieds if you like."

"I understand."

"Do you?" Reid let go of her arm, stuffing his hands in his coat pockets. "Yes, I think you do. You've been very good to me, Sylvie. Better than I deserve. I'm sorry."

Suddenly there were tears in her eyes. She swallowed. "It's time for you to go. Right now."

"Okay." He caught her gaze one last time. Gave her a sad smile. Then turned away.

Watching him drive off from the vantage point of her front window, Sylvie imagined her mother standing beside her.

"You did the right thing," her mother would have said.

"Yes."

GEORGIA WAS INTO the third hour of her show and fielding so many calls, she didn't have a second to spare. You'd think people would have better things to do on Christmas Eve than listen to her program, but no. From the way her phone was lighting up, half the city must have tuned in.

She clipped her notes for the next segment to the board, then turned to read an e-mail that had just come through.

"Yikes!" Her elbow caught the insulated mug and toppled it over. Hot chocolate streamed across the desk toward her control board.

She grabbed her sweater from the back of her

chair and quickly mopped up the liquid before it could do any damage. Then she looked at the dark-brown stain on her red sweater with displeasure.

She glanced up to see Larry waving frantically. The last song was over and she was up. Quickly she flipped on the record button.

"This is Georgia and you're listening to *Seattle after Midnight*. It's just past three in the morning on the night before Christmas." She paused a second to catch her breath and regroup her thoughts. "Tonight I'm wondering, not if you believe in Santa, but do you believe in love? Here's what I've been hearing…."

During the last break, she'd edited a string of calls into one continuous recording. With a nod from Larry, she queued it in.

"Hi, this is Sandra." The voice was female and very bubbly. "I'm calling to say that I do believe in love. Two hours ago my boyfriend gave me the most beautiful ring. We're getting married in the spring!"

Next up was a male caller. "Georgia? Cameron here. You asked if I believe in love? I'm sitting alone in my new house on Christmas Eve because my wife of three years just left me—along with a string of debts it'll take me forever to pay off. So, no, I do not believe in love. Not now and probably not ever."

"I'm Melanie-Lynn and I'm calling from the Northwest Hospital to tell you I just had a baby girl. She's in my arms right now. She's seven pounds and absolutely perfect. My husband is holding my hand

and he looks so proud and so happy. So yes, Georgia, I do believe in love. You bet I do."

"Ah, isn't that sweet?" Georgia said, speaking live. "Congratulations Melanie-Lynn and Sandra and all my other listeners with happy news tonight. As for Cameron… I think you need a good song. Here's something by Bob James. He's joined here by his daughter Hillary who does vocals. 'Storm Warnings' going out to Cameron tonight."

She queued in the song, then took a deep breath. She opened a desk drawer and pulled out a Wet Wipes to clean the side of her mug and the remaining stickiness on her desk. She trashed the wipe, then put her damp, soiled sweater into a plastic bag.

The little accident had been annoying, but it didn't change the fact that her show was strong tonight—perhaps the strongest it had ever been. She could feel it in her bones.

And yet, her own mood was low. She couldn't shake her overwhelming feeling of anxiety. And a strange weariness, too, that she didn't understand.

"Georgia? You there?"

She put her hands on her earphones and concentrated on Larry's voice. "Where else would I be?" she answered lightly.

"This is the best show, yet, Georgia. The phone lines are flooded."

She glanced at him through the glass partition. He smiled and gave her a thumbs-up.

Syndication. A country-wide broadcast. Tonight, all her goals seemed tantalizingly within reach.

She reached for her hot chocolate—there was still a little left—lukewarm, but rich and sweet. She wished Larry had bought her coffee, instead. Tonight she really needed the caffeine. She was so tired. She indulged in a big, long yawn, then tried to focus on her program.

PIERCE SHUT DOWN the office computer with a yawn. It had taken hours of searching but he'd finally found the phone number for the woman he thought was Monty's stepdaughter, as well as the number for another one of Larry's old girlfriends. It was obviously too early to call either woman now, but he'd contact them in the morning. He didn't care if it was Christmas Day.

"Tell me, Seattle. Do you believe in love? Give me a call. I'm sitting here, waiting to hear from you. This is Georgia at KXPG and you're listening to *Seattle after Midnight*...."

He closed his eyes, then rubbed them. God how they burned. He wished Georgia was in this room with him right now, not sitting in some faraway studio talking to strangers as if they were her most intimate friends.

Now you're jealous of her radio program? Man, you've got it bad.

He did have it bad. Real bad. So bad he was ready

to go crawling to her. Except she'd had it with him. He'd seen it in her eyes today. She wasn't putting up with his bullshit anymore. She was moving on.

She'd probably get back together with her old boyfriend when she went home for Christmas.

Just thinking about that possibility was torture.

Pierce stood up and the cat, who'd been curled in his lap, sleeping, jumped indignantly to the floor.

"Sorry, cat. Find yourself some better place to spend the night." He wandered out to the reception area and settled on the overstuffed love seat meant for waiting clients. Robin's tree glowed warmly in the dark. The damn lights had been left on again.

The cat followed him and jumped on his lap once more. She banged her head against his hand until finally he started to scratch her under the chin.

The little reprobate then had the nerve to purr.

He relaxed his head back, caught up in the music playing on the radio. Georgia's last words were still echoing in his head. *Do you believe in love?*

Why had she posed that question tonight, when he was struggling so hard to remind himself that love was not part of his repertoire? People had to be loved as children, to know how to love as adults. How many times had Cass told him that? She'd worked so hard to "heal" him. Without success.

Why? Because he wasn't capable of love? Or because Cass just hadn't been the right woman?

Time flashed backward in his head. He remembered two years ago. Sitting by a hospital bed, holding her hand. She'd been in a deep coma and the doctors had told him that the next couple of hours were crucial. He'd squeezed her fingers and prayed to see some sign that his wife was coming back to life, but there'd been nothing.

Not that day, nor the next, nor the day after.

Finally the doctors had asked for permission to pull the plugs on the machines that were keeping oxygen and fluids in her system and her heart pumping. Pierce had made that decision together with Cass's parents, who'd driven from Spokane on Christmas morning, after he'd called to give them the news.

He thought of Jan and Wilfred and wondered how they were doing. Did they now find Christmas as impossible as he did? But they had two other children, both married with kids of their own. That must have helped. Given them reason to move on.

They'd sent him a Christmas card this year. Last year, too. In both, Jan had issued an invitation to join the family for the holidays.

"You shouldn't be alone,…" Jan had written.

Yet, hadn't he always been alone? Even when he'd been married. He sank deeper into the love seat. On the radio a sad, haunting melody began to play.

"What are you thinking?" In his mind he could hear Cass's plaintive voice. "You never talk to me." His wife's voice changed, turned into someone else's. "Do you believe in love?"

This was Georgia. He could picture her sweet face, remember her gentle touch.

"Do you believe in love, Pierce? Tell me you believe in love."

The jumble of memories, faces and voices faded. With the Christmas lights still glowing on the artificial tree and the office cat snuggled on his lap, Pierce finally slept.

CHAPTER SIXTEEN

"HI, GEORGIA. I was at the mall on Sunday. You wrapped a present for me. Do you remember?"

Pierce jerked awake. The cat yowled and jumped to the floor. He crossed the room in three long strides, then turned up the radio.

"Is this Jack?" Georgia asked, sounding bemused.

"You touched my hand when you passed the present back to me. I just wanted to say Merry Christmas to you."

"Merry Christmas to you, too."

Pierce could tell Georgia had been caught off guard. What the hell was the matter with Larry? He wasn't supposed to be putting through any calls from Jack.

"Courtney doesn't care if I live or die."

"You know what, Jack? Who cares what Courtney thinks. I'll bet every one of my listeners tonight thinks she's a fool. You can do better than Courtney. Remember that Jack.

"And now," she continued, "as we come up to four in morning, it's time for another Christmas song...."

Georgia's voice sounded funny. As if she'd been drinking, which was out of the question, Pierce knew.

As "The Twelve Days of Christmas" started to play—one of the world's most annoying carols in Pierce's opinion—Pierce reached for the button to turn off the radio.

He paused as he heard the first line of lyrics. *The first day of Christmas...* That had been in one of Georgia's notes, hadn't it?

He grabbed the file and flipped pages until he found the note that had been delivered at the mall. *On the first day of Christmas my true love gave to me...* not a partridge in a pear tree, but one perfect red rose.

Was that where the stalker had gotten the idea for twelve roses? From the song that was now playing, in its endless fashion, on his radio?

But if that was the case, wouldn't it make sense for the last rose to be delivered on Christmas?

Today.

Hell. He yanked the extension cord from the wall. The Christmas lights blinked out and the office turned dark. He grabbed his coat and left, locking the door behind him.

God, how could he have been so complacent, assuming that with Georgia headed for South Dakota after her show, everything would be fine?

The stalker was going to make his move tonight. Pierce was sure of it. Which had to mean the stalker could only be one of two people. Pierce cursed himself again for being so foolish. For putting Georgia's life on the line.

Before heading to the KXPG office, he went to his desk and dialed the phone number he'd only just discovered on the Internet tonight. She could help, he thought. She might have the one piece of evidence he needed to nail this sucker.

AT FOUR in the morning, Sylvie was startled out of sleep by a phone call.

Reid, she thought. *He's changed his mind.*

She reached for the phone with a sad heart, knowing the conversation wouldn't be easy. An affair with a married man had seemed so perfect at the beginning. So romantic and exciting, filled with drama and secrets. Everything upfront at the beginning, so no one would be hurt.

But people didn't operate that way, and even lighthearted affairs had to eventually lead somewhere. In the end, no matter how hard you tried to avoid it, the hurting came. She suspected her own heart would heal rapidly. But Reid and his wife—for them the suffering was only beginning. She had to help Reid find the strength to get through it.

But it wasn't Reid who was calling. It was a man she'd never met, a man she hadn't even known existed.

But he knew her. And he knew about her mother, too.

He explained the situation so quickly, she had to ask him to repeat himself several times.

Finally she understood. And deep inside, she knew he was right.

"Yes," she said. "I think he did."

"Can you meet me?" he asked. "I think he might kill someone else tonight."

"I'll take a cab. I'll be there as fast as I can."

WITH MUSIC PLAYING on air, Georgia listened to the recording of her last call again. It was Jack. Jack saying he'd met her at the mall last Sunday. She put her fingers on her temples and closed her eyes, trying to match his voice to one of the faces she'd met on Sunday.

Even though she was tired, it didn't take long to recall the adolescent who had asked her to wrap a book for his mother. A tall guy, with terrible acne. What had he said his name was? She remembered being reminded of a favorite oldies TV show when he said it. That didn't help at all. There were dozens of old TV shows that she'd watched as a kid.

She tried to concentrate on what she was going to say when the song ended, but her thoughts kept circling back to Jack. If she remembered correctly, it was right after she'd wrapped his gift that she'd found the last two roses.

Had Jack put them there?

She wished she could remember his name. What

was the matter with her tonight? She couldn't think straight.

She glanced at her monitor. Five seconds until the song ended. She buzzed through to Larry. He shouldn't have put through that call from Jack, but she'd talk to him about it later. "Play some music to cover me for a while, okay?"

Then she reached for the phone to call Pierce.

IT TOOK PIERCE ten minutes to drive to the station building. He parked right by the entrance, then sprang out of his car to ring security.

No response. Peering into the foyer, he could see the security desk. Monty Greenfield wasn't there.

Pierce dashed back to his car. At first he was reassured by the sound of Georgia's program playing on the radio. Then it occurred to him that he hadn't actually heard her voice for a while. Just songs and prerecorded jingles. Usually Georgia talked and played phone calls between every song.

Suddenly certain that something was very wrong, Pierce reached into his jacket for his cell phone. He had to call the cops. But he couldn't find his phone. It must have slipped from his pocket when he'd been dozing on the couch.

CONCENTRATING was becoming increasingly difficult for Georgia. Worse, she was unaccountably sleepy. Though she worked impossible hours, this had never happened to her before. She programmed in some prerecorded calls, then asked Larry to cover for her again while she went to the washroom. She took a last drink of hot chocolate—which was almost cold now—then left her studio.

She hadn't been able to get hold of Pierce. She was dying to tell him her theory about Jack. He was the one bringing the roses after all. They didn't have to worry. It was only Jack.

But maybe Pierce didn't care anymore. He hadn't answered his phone. She wouldn't see him again until after she returned from South Dakota on the twenty-seventh. Possibly she wouldn't see him even then. Jack would have tired of his game by then. If she wasn't getting any more roses or notes, what excuse would she have to give Pierce a call? He'd made it clear he had no intention of phoning *her*.

Georgia washed her hands with cool water, then splashed her face as well, hoping to revive herself. What was the matter with her? She looked at her reflection and frowned.

Something wasn't right, but she couldn't say what.

Back at her desk, she tried to inject some enthusiasm into her voice.

"Georgia here and we're coming to the end of our Christmas Eve program. This is your last chance to tell me why you believe in love. Maybe it's something that's happening in your life right now. Like Alicia Keys, maybe you're 'Fallin'...."

She queued in the song, then sank her head to the desk. It was too late for her. She'd already fallen in love. Unfortunately she'd chosen a man who didn't believe in the word.

"Are you okay?" Larry asked over the headphones.

"Fine. Just tired."

"Yeah, I know how you feel. Only twenty-five minutes to go. You going to make it?"

Georgia forced her head off the desk. He sounded concerned, but she knew better. He was probably hoping she would screw up. He'd really love it if she did that.

Determinedly, she tried to focus once more on the play list. She was going to finish this program if it killed her.

PIERCE HAD his eye on the dark Audi before it turned into the station's parking lot. The young male driver seemed indecisive, first driving past the parking lot entrance, then circling the block and coming by again. This time he nosed his expensive vehicle into the lot and cautiously explored up one aisle, then down another. Finally the Audi came to rest in a space not far from the main door.

Pierce was bolt upright in his seat by now. He'd spent enough hours in this parking lot to know this car didn't belong to any of the employees who worked at this time of day.

Pierce's suspicions grew when the driver didn't get out of his car. A couple minutes passed, and Pierce couldn't stand it anymore. Quietly he let himself out into the night. Sticking to the shadows, he ran in zigzag fashion across the pavement.

Approaching from the rear, he caught the silhouette of the young man in the driver's seat. As he'd thought, no one else was in the car. The driver was holding something to the side of his head.

A cell phone.

Was he calling Georgia right now?

The idea infuriated him. He made a final dash for the car and grasped the door handle. In a flash he had the door open.

The driver gaped at him. He dropped his phone and held up his hands.

"I don't have any money."

Jesus. He was just a kid. Didn't even look old enough to drive.

"Hi, Jack," Pierce said. He reached across the boy—frozen in his seat, eyes round and terrified—and picked up the phone, which had fallen on the console.

Sure enough, he saw Georgia's station number on the display. He held it to his ear. "Georgia?"

No answer.

"Her p-producer has me on hold," the kid said.

Pierce stared at him, trying to remember where he'd seen him before. Then it hit him. This guy had been in the lineup for gift wrapping at the mall last Sunday. Of course. He'd said as much in his last phone call to Georgia.

"Get out of your car. Lock it up and give me the keys."

The boy did as he was asked, though his whole body was trembling with fear. "Are you going to steal my mom's car?"

His mom's car. Figured. "Does she know you're out with it?"

"N-not exactly."

"Do you even have a valid driver's license?"

"Um, a learner's permit. Want to see it?"

"That's okay." He took measure of the kid again. Didn't seem like much of a threat. Still, he'd been at the mall, been phoning Georgia, and what the hell was he doing at the KXPG parking lot at quarter to five on Christmas morning?

"Come on, let's go sit in my car. We need to talk."

Since Pierce still had his keys, the kid realized he had no choice but to follow. "You a cop?"

"Used to be."

"Am I going to get in trouble? Are you going to call my mom?"

"Just get in the car." Pierce stopped at his Nissan, then nodded his head toward the passenger side. Once inside he started the motor. It was damn chilly tonight. If the precipitation ever did arrive, they'd probably end up with snow as predicted.

"So tell me everything," he said. "Who are you and what are you doing here? Why were you calling Georgia?"

The boy seemed perfectly willing to talk. "I'm Brady Walsh and I live with my mom in Madison Park."

Given the posh car, it figured he lived in a rich neighborhood. "And why were you calling Georgia?"

"I listen to her show all the time, man. She's really cool. I like talking to her." He shrugged.

"Why did you go to the mall on Sunday to meet her?"

"I'm like, a fan, okay? I didn't do anything wrong. I paid five bucks and got her to wrap my mom's Christmas present for me."

The kid seemed on the level. Pierce let his shoulders relax a little. "Why aren't you at home in bed? It's almost Christmas morning."

Brady shrugged and for the first time, dropped his gaze from Pierce's. "It won't be Christmas morning at our house. We didn't even put up a tree this year."

Poor kid. Even as he had the thought, Pierce caught himself. Despite all the sentimental media hype at this time of year, most families' problems got worse over Christmas, not better.

Before he started feeling too sorry for this boy, he had to make sure he wasn't a threat to Georgia.

"Have you followed Georgia before?"

"I've never followed her. I went to the mall on Sunday, but that was advertised on the radio. I guess I showed up here tonight, because I really didn't know where else to go."

The kid looked and sounded miserable. "You ever send her any flowers?"

"No." His head shot up. "Does she like flowers?"

Pierce covered his unexpected smile with his hand. "You know what we're going to do here? You're going to give your mom a call and have her come and pick you up. You shouldn't be driving without a license. You could get into some real trouble, especially if you were in an accident. You ever been in trouble with the law before?"

The kid's eyes turned as round as the premium tires on his mother's Audi. "No."

He was so obviously exactly what he seemed. A naïve young kid, torn up inside because of family troubles.

"Well, let's keep it that way, okay? Let's go back to your car to use your phone." He opened his door and the boy followed.

In the Audi, the kid dialed home. As he was trying to explain his predicament to his undoubtedly sleepy and confused mother, Pierce noticed a taxi pull up to the entrance of the KXPG building. A redhead stepped out. She had a trench coat wrapped around her thin body and seemed tense and anxious.

Good. She'd shown up. He'd been afraid she would write him off as a kook and go back to sleep.

"You wait here for your mom, okay? I need to check out something." With the Audi keys still in his possession, he left the car and ran toward the waiting woman.

IF GEORGIA HADN'T known better, she would have thought she was drunk. She could tell Larry suspected so, too.

"You were slurring your words a little in that last segment."

"I was?"

Larry took off his headphones and strode out of the control room. Two seconds later he was at her door. "How about we use some prerecorded material to finish up the show? It's Christmas—I say we get out of here and go home. You have a flight to catch, right?"

Georgia fought the deep desire to slouch into her chair and go to sleep. "I do."

"How are you getting to the airport? Do you want a ride?"

Decent of him to offer. "Thanks. But I'm—" For a moment she forgot what she'd been about to say. Then it came to her "—taking a cab."

Larry frowned. "I don't think you're just tired. Are you coming down with something? Your face looks a little red."

"Maybe a cold," she fibbed. This was like no cold she'd ever had.

"Let me call you that cab." Larry picked up her phone and dialed a number. "He says he can be here in ten minutes. I'll take you to the front desk. You can wait with Monty."

She didn't think she could walk without stumbling and she did not want Larry to see her like that. He'd definitely think she'd been drinking; she could see the doubt in his eyes. But all she'd had tonight was an apple and the hot chocolate he'd given her.

She filled her lungs with air and made a huge effort to sound clearheaded. "You go ahead, Larry. I need to do a few things before I leave. Have a merry Christmas, okay? And thanks again for the hot chocolate and the mug."

Larry looked relieved to be on his way. "You, too," he said. "And you should probably thank Monty for the hot chocolate. It was his idea I get you something. He even ran down to the coffee shop to pick it up for me."

With that Larry left and the moment he was gone, Georgia dropped her head to the desktop. Oh, God, how was she going to pull herself together to get to the airport? She didn't think she could make it to the front door on her own.

If only she could get hold of Pierce...

She tried his cell phone again, his home number, his office. No answer. Where the heck was he?

Maybe Monty would help her downstairs. He wouldn't think she'd been drinking and even if he did, he wouldn't tell management about his suspicions, as she worried Larry might have done.

She reached for the phone again, to dial the local extension for security.

But then the door opened and Monty stepped into her studio.

"Thank God you're here," she said to him. "I feel terrible. I don't know what's wrong."

"I'll take care of you."

Something in his voice caught her attention and she tried to focus on him. He sounded different. More confident, stronger… And he looked different, too. He had one hand behind his back. What…?

She guessed the truth a split second before he pulled the rose out from behind his back and presented it to her.

"I'll take care of you, Georgia. Always."

CHAPTER SEVENTEEN

SYLVIE MOREAU stepped back from the strange man who'd suddenly emerged from a shadow in the parking lot. It occurred to her that coming out by herself before the crack of dawn to meet a man she didn't know wasn't the smartest move she could have made.

He was tall and well built, with dark hair and a lean angry face. She swallowed and prayed this was the man who'd phoned her. And that he'd been telling the truth when he'd said he had information about her former stepfather.

"Are you Pierce Harding?"

"I am. Sylvie Moreau?"

She stepped forward to take his hand. And was reassured when she saw a flash of kindness in his dark eyes.

"Your mother was Elizabeth Moreau?" he asked. "I spoke to one of the nurses who was on duty the night she died. She said the circumstances of your mother's illness were not clear-cut."

"That's right. My mother had diabetes, which

she'd always kept carefully under control. The idea that she could have made a mistake with her insulin—I just don't believe it. I'm sure she was poisoned. By the husband who just happened to take out a large life insurance policy on her after their marriage."

Pierce shook his head sympathetically.

"I should have been suspicious at the time," Sylvie said, "but I wasn't that smart. Now my mother is dead and it's all Monty Greenfield's fault."

"YOU'RE THE ONE who's been sending me the roses?" If Georgia hadn't been feeling so queasy she might have laughed. Monty Greenfield, the security guard she'd baked cookies for and felt so sorry for, had been stalking her and scaring her half to death.

He held out the twelfth rose to her.

She didn't want to touch it, but she took it anyway, noticing that this was the first rose she'd received that didn't come with a note.

Well, of course there was no need for a note since this one was hand-delivered.

"What is this? Some kind of game?"

Monty's features shifted, transforming him from a sweet, middle-aged widower to an ugly, dangerous stranger. "No game, Georgia. I used to listen to you when you worked in Sioux Falls. When I heard you were coming to Seattle, I hustled to get myself this job. I've been planning for this moment a long, long time."

Up until that moment, she hadn't been truly frightened. Monty wouldn't hurt her. She would have sworn he was harmless.

But what she saw in his face, what he'd just said, was terrifying. There was something very wrong with this man.

"I was in the mall on Sunday, too," Monty said. "You didn't notice me, did you?"

"In the coffee shop? Reading the paper?"

"That was me."

"Oh, Monty. Why didn't you tell me sooner? Why all the secrecy?"

"It was too soon, Georgia. You needed to receive all twelve roses before I revealed my identity to you. And I wanted the last rose to be delivered on Christmas morning." His gaze swept to the travel mug on her desk. He picked it up and saw that it was empty. "You must be feeling very tired, my dear. And confused."

Finally, she understood what had happened. "You drugged my drink. Why did you do that? I thought we were friends."

"Just a little Valium. Enough so you would be nice and relaxed."

Valium? Wasn't that available by prescription only? Of course, he was a pharmacist. That would be no obstacle. "How much did you put in my drink?"

"Don't worry. I know what I'm doing. By the time we get to the chalet, you'll have slept it off."

"What chalet?"

"I've bought us a place in the mountains, very rustic, very isolated. We'll have everything we need, for a very long time."

"I'm not going to any chalet with you."

"Oh, yes you are. I have a lot of money, Georgia. My second insurance claim came through yesterday. Just in time for Christmas."

He'd said *second* insurance claim. So he'd made money off his first wife, too. Was Pierce right? Had he married sick women hoping they would die? Oh, my Lord, maybe he'd *helped* them to die.

Could Monty be a murderer?

She felt a fear so strong it paralyzed her. Then her mind took over. *Talk, Georgia. It's your only chance. Talk to him. Get him talking back....*

"Monty, let's be rational for a minute. You can't make me go to that chalet with you. I was supposed to be flying home today. My parents are going to freak out when I don't show up. They'll call the police and the police will figure out you're missing, too."

"It doesn't matter. They'll never find us. I've got everything covered, you don't need to worry." He advanced slowly, his eyes burning intensely.

"I am worried, because I don't think this is such a good plan. Let me phone—"

"No. No phone calls. Just be quiet and rest." He checked the time on the big clock above her desk with a worried scowl. "I don't understand this. You should be sleeping by now."

Thank God she'd spilled some of that drink.

"Don't look at me like that. Don't be afraid. I'm going to treat you like a princess. You'll see. We're going to be very happy together."

Georgia couldn't bear to meet his eyes, to see the hungry, possessive way he was looking at her.

"You're a wonderful person, Georgia. So pretty and kind."

And you're a monster. Even with the evidence before her eyes, she could hardly believe it. Monty had always been so nice. So thoughtful.

"I had no idea you felt this way about me, Monty. I thought we were friends."

"First time I heard you on the radio, I knew you were special. I looked up your picture on the radio station's Web site and when I saw your face, I knew you were the one I'd been waiting for. The one I'd made all my money for."

"Money? You mean the insurance policies on your wives?"

"I worked damn hard for that money. You don't know what I put up with. I screened all my customers carefully, looking for just the right candidate."

"Is *that* how you picked your wives?"

He nodded. "Elizabeth Moreau was widowed and wealthy and a diabetic—the perfect combination. I knew exactly how to manipulate her drugs to make her death seem completely natural. No one even questioned me about that. But after a few weeks, once the shock of her mother's death had passed, I could tell her daughter was getting suspicious and so I moved to a new neighborhood, got a different job."

Georgia stared, speechless.

"I met Nancy at that pharmacy. And I was just as clever the second time. I knew the right drug to give her to shut down her entire respiratory system. Given her long-term health problems, no one questioned her death, either."

Those poor women. "But why do it again if you had the insurance money from the first time?"

"I wanted a million, but I was too smart to be greedy. The larger the policy, the more likely the insurance company was going to ask questions. Mistakes like that create too much suspicion."

She tried to back away from him, but dizziness made her stumble.

"I told you to stop looking at me like that," Monty commanded. "I earned this money. You wouldn't believe what I had to put up with to get it. Sick, whining women…God, after all these years of sacrifice, don't you think I deserve a beautiful sweet wife for the rest of my life?"

"Oh, Monty." He was insane. He'd killed Elizabeth and Nancy. "Are you going to kill me, too?"

"You're going to be fine. I'm not going to let anything bad happen to you."

Oh, God. He was so crazy. Didn't he think getting drugged and abducted against her will was bad? "I have to catch the six-forty-five flight to Sioux Falls—"

Monty's face tightened with anger. "Haven't you been listening to me? You're not going to Sioux Falls. You're staying with me. We're going to be together forever. Come on, I've got my car in the basement."

There was a parkade beneath the building, though she never used it. The rates were too high and the concrete labyrinth too spooky to use during late-night hours.

"I can't make it all the way to the basement. Pick me up at the front door," she pleaded. If she could just get to that waiting taxi, then she could call the police.

"No. We're doing this my way." Monty's voice was tight and hard. He grabbed her by the hand, but when he pulled her forward, her knees collapsed and she fell to the floor, hitting her head on the metal file cabinet beside her.

"Georgia!" Monty dropped to his knees, beside her. "Are you okay? Come on, get up. Open your eyes. Oh, God, you're bleeding. This wasn't part of my plan."

As Georgia's show came to its conclusion—without any live segments from Georgia at all—Pierce's sense of unease grew to full-scale alarm. The security guard was still missing. Where the hell was Greenfield? Brady Walsh, sitting in the Audi waiting for his mother, was watching him curiously.

Pierce leaned on the buzzer, though he suspected it was a futile effort.

"How do you know Monty Greenfield?" Sylvie Moreau asked, observing his actions with curiosity.

"I've just recently started checking into his past. He hooked up with another woman after your mother. You won't be surprised to hear that she died recently."

"Oh, my God." Her hands flew to her face. "Did he kill her, too?"

"I haven't been able to reach her doctors so far, but I did get to question one of the nurses. Nancy had asthma, and I think it's possible Monty gave her a drug that was incompatible with her asthma medication."

"And now he's after someone else?"

Pierce tried the buzzer again, then a futile yank at the door. "He's changed his modus operandi a little, but yeah, he's after someone else."

The woman I love.

He couldn't say the words out loud, but he could think them. They were the truth, after all.

"Is she in there?"

As Pierce nodded, a second taxi pulled up to the building, from a different company than the first one.

"Did you call him?" Pierce asked Sylvie.

"No. I wasn't sure how long I'd be."

This had to be the cab to take Georgia to the airport. Then, where was she? Was Monty giving her the twelfth rose right this minute?

But Larry Sizemore was still in there.

Only he wasn't, Pierce suddenly realized. Through the glass door he saw a small man dash down the stairs and head for the exit.

At least now he'd get inside and find Georgia.

Pierce waited by the door and the moment Sizemore opened it, he grabbed the handle and held fast.

"Excuse me?" Sizemore froze in place, glaring at Pierce suspiciously. "You don't work in this building. I'm afraid I can't let you enter."

"Just try to stop me. Is Georgia still in her studio?"

"I'm not sure. I stopped to leave a little gift at the desk of…a friend of mine."

Rachel Masterson, Pierce assumed from the flush creeping up Sizemore's neck. He turned back to Sylvie. "When the police get here, tell them to come to the third floor. Tell them it's an emergency."

As he dashed toward the stairs, he was surprised to hear footsteps following him. He turned to see Sylvie trying to catch up.

"Wait for the police outside," he told her.

"No," Sylvie said. "I'm coming with you."

He wanted to argue, but there wasn't time. He ran up the stairs, Sylvie right behind him. On the third floor, he paused to get his bearings.

"This way." He opened a door and led her down the hall to the news bullpen. The lights were off and he had to feel his way with a hand to the wall.

"Do you think he's dangerous?" he asked in a whisper.

Sylvie hesitated, then replied quietly, "Yes. I think he's crazy. He could do anything."

Pierce held a finger to his mouth, then stealthily followed the wall as it cornered into Georgia's studio. With the lights on in the small room, the sealed window acted as a perfect one-way mirror. Pierce didn't see anyone at first. Then he realized Greenfield was on the floor, crouched over Georgia. Her eyes were closed, and she wasn't moving. There was blood on the side of her head.

Georgia, Georgia! He wanted to burst into the room and gather her in his arms.

But Greenfield would be armed, while Pierce didn't have a gun on him. He glanced back at Sylvie, standing several feet away, her eyes round with apprehension. This woman, he realized, could very well be his secret weapon.

He motioned her over to the producer's control room, then whispered what he wanted her to do.

"Can you handle that? Remember, give me twenty seconds."

She nodded yes, then quietly slipped inside the other room.

Pierce stationed himself outside Georgia's studio. He gripped the door handle, praying Monty hadn't thought to lock it.

GEORGIA MOANED. Her head ached and her mouth was desperately dry. She opened her eyes to find Monty's face right next to hers and almost screamed.

Oh, God. Everything came back to her in one awful rush. The twelfth rose, the drugged hot chocolate, Monty Greenfield's terrible plan. She pushed her upper body up, supporting her weight with her arms.

Monty handed her a wad of tissues. Shocked, she realized that the dampness she'd felt on her head was blood.

"Are you okay?"

He had to be kidding. "No, Monty, I'm not okay. It's Christmas morning. I'm supposed to be flying home to my family. Instead, I think you're going to have to take me to the hospital." Her head throbbed and there was so much blood, the tissues were already soaked through.

"No hospital. It's just a superficial wound. Trust me, Georgia. You'll like the chalet and it's completely stocked with food and everything. I've even got a tree and Christmas presents. Stand up. Lean on me. I'm parked underground, so we can—"

As he spoke, he was pulling at her to stand.

"Get away from me! I'm not—"

He slapped her across the face, and a jolting pain slashed through her head.

"Don't fight me, Georgia. I told you I have everything planned. Don't make me hurt you."

He put a hand to his belt, and suddenly she saw his gun. She'd never really noticed it before, even though he'd probably worn it every day to work. She cringed as he began to pull the weapon out of his holster.

But at just that moment, a movement in Larry's control room caught Monty's attention. He swung his head to the left. "What the hell?"

Georgia froze at the sight of a woman staring back at them—at Monty, actually—from the other side of the window. The woman was like a ghost, her face expressionless, unmoving.

"Elizabeth?" Monty murmured. "No, it can't be. Not Elizabeth…"

The door to Georgia's studio slammed open, hitting the wall with a bang.

Pierce burst inside and lunged for Monty. The security guard still had his hand on his gun and he tried to swing it out, but Pierce intercepted him, felling the older man with a powerful blow to the head.

Drawing back his fist, Pierce watched the man hit the floor with a thud. Monty moaned as Pierce pulled the gun from the holster.

The woman from the control room suddenly appeared in Georgia's studio. "You bastard," she said to Monty. "This time you're going to pay for what you did to my mother."

Mother? Monty had said Nancy had no family. So this had to be his first victim's daughter.

Pierce handed the gun to Sylvie. "Keep an eye on him for a minute."

"My pleasure." Sylvie's hand was steady as she trained the gun on the KXPG security guard.

Georgia attempted to stand as she held the blood-soaked tissues to the side of her head. Feeling dampness on her cheeks, she brought up her free hand to brush away the blood and was surprised to find the liquid clear.

She was crying.

"Baby." Pierce crouched in front of her, his face stricken. "What did he do to you?"

Tenderly he brushed back her hair to look at the wound. He grabbed fresh tissues, a whole box of them, and held the compress to her head.

Georgia leaned into his chest. "He drugged my hot chocolate…hit me…." Her left cheek still felt as if it were burning. There'd be a welt. "My parents…so worried…"

"I'll call and let them know. Let's just wait here a few minutes…."

Georgia could hear sirens now. She closed her eyes and sighed, Pierce's heart pounding solidly against her ear. She heard the woman speak to Pierce.

She thought it was something like, "Don't worry. She's going to be okay."

Then she finally gave in to the drugs and drifted away.

CHAPTER EIGHTEEN

WHILE PIERCE kept the gun trained on Monty, Sylvie ran down to the lobby to let the police into the building. Once the cops had assessed the situation and ensured the scene was under control, the paramedics streamed inside. Two of them began a careful examination of Georgia.

Throughout it all—the examination by the paramedics, the questioning by the police—Pierce remained at Georgia's side, holding her hand. He only left her once—to contact her parents and assure them that though she had missed her flight, she was fine and would call them herself shortly.

"Vitals are normal," one of the paramedics reported to Pierce. "Her head wound is superficial and has stopped bleeding. The reason she seems so groggy right now is because of the Valium. We found the pill container in the security guard's pocket. Only two pills were missing."

"She's so sleepy."

"The sedative effect should start wearing off in a

couple of hours. We could certainly take her to the hospital to keep an eye on her."

Throughout all this, Georgia felt Pierce's strong fingers and warm palm, anchoring her as she fought against the dizzying effect of the drugs, and the emotional drain of the entire situation.

Monty Greenfield had sent her the roses. She couldn't get over it.

And he had killed those poor women. Women he had once professed to love, as tonight he had claimed to love her.

He'd continued that claim, right until the moment the police escorted him out of her studio. "I love you, Georgia…." Would she ever get the sound of his voice, profaning those words, out of her mind?

"Maybe we should take her to the hospital," Pierce said.

"But it's Christmas," Georgia moaned.

"You could keep an eye on her at home," one of the paramedics said. He gave Pierce a list of symptoms to watch out for. "Bring her directly to emergency if anything seems wrong."

Next, Pierce fended off the police. They agreed to wait until the following day for a more detailed report.

"Ready to go?" Pierce asked her, as the paramedics filed out of the room.

"Please." Georgia leaned heavily against him on her way out of the studio.

The red-haired woman took Georgia's free arm

and helped Pierce lead her out of the building. Cold air swept over them all as they stepped out to the frosty sidewalk. Pierce moved protectively closer to Georgia.

"It's freezing." The woman wrapped her coat tightly across her chest. Georgia still didn't know who she was.

"I'm Georgia Lamont."

The woman's smile didn't reach her eyes. "I'm Sylvie Moreau. My mother was—" Her gaze fell away as she was unable to complete her sentence.

"Your mother was Monty's first wife?" Georgia guessed.

Sylvie nodded. "Yes. I'd like the chance to tell you the whole story sometime. When you're feeling better. I suppose I ought to call a—"

She broke off her sentence and Georgia turned to see what had silenced her. Two people approached from the parking lot. A woman in her forties and a tall adolescent boy.

The teenager from the mall, Georgia realized in surprise. Jack.

"Oh, hell, I forgot all about you, kid." Pierce reached a hand into his pocket and pulled out a set of car keys, which he passed to the woman. "We've had a little drama here, as you can see. I'm Pierce Harding, and this is Georgia Lamont from KXPG radio and Sylvie Moreau."

The woman nodded, though she still appeared

puzzled. "I'm Annette Walsh. This is my son, Brady. Though I gather he has already met some of you."

"Brady?" Of course, from *The Brady Bunch*. She should have remembered. "It's good to see you again, though I'll always think of you as Jack."

"Jack?" His mother put a hand to her mouth. She swung her eyes from Georgia to her son.

"It's my middle name," he said to Georgia. Then he turned to his mother. "I used it whenever I called Georgia on the radio."

Annette was silent for a moment, then she looked back at Georgia. "Jack was also my husband's name. Brady's father." She swallowed, as if there were more to the story that she didn't want to tell. There was.

"Jack died last July. I've—we've—been having trouble getting by without him. I had no idea Brady was going out at night with my car. Thanks for finding him," she said to Pierce.

Georgia reached out to Brady, putting her hand on his shoulder. "This is what all those phone calls were about, weren't they? Not Courtney." Courtney had been an excuse. A diversion. "I'm sorry about your father, Brady."

Tears were streaming from his mother's eyes and Georgia couldn't stop the tears pooling in her own eyes, too.

"It's going to be a difficult Christmas," Annette said.

Yes. A difficult Christmas. Georgia thought of Annette and Brady, missing their husband and father. Fred, alone in his duplex. Monty in a cell. Her parents not setting out her stocking for the first Christmas of her life.

And Pierce. But then, Christmas had always been difficult for him.

"I should be going," Sylvie Moreau said. "I'll just call a cab."

"We can give you a ride," Annette offered.

Before they left, Pierce collected phone numbers. Then he escorted Georgia to his car. As he opened the door for her, Georgia noticed it had started to snow.

GEORGIA FELL ASLEEP on the ride home. Pierce carried her from the car to her bed. He sat in the chair by the window, alternately watching her sleep, and staring out at the view. The falling snow was quietly transforming the neighborhood.

The way Georgia had transformed his life.

Nothing looked the same to him anymore. Nothing.

The digital display by her bed gave a soft click as the time switched from 7:59 to 8:00 a.m. Georgia had been motionless since her head settled on her pillow. He went over to check her more closely, the gentle rise and fall of her chest, the warmth and color in her cheeks—though a bruise was rapidly rising in one of them.

She was fine.

He thought of her parents. Now that things had calmed down he should give them another call. He went downstairs so he wouldn't wake Georgia.

In the living room a gorgeous white pine had been decorated with dozens of colored balls and frosty white lights. Though he usually found Christmas decorations cheesy, for some reason the sight of this tree—and the pretty quilted stocking that Georgia had placed next to it—gave him a choked up, sentimental feeling.

The year Cass had died, she'd already set up the tree in their home. He'd left it sitting there all January. By the time he'd taken it down, in February, it had been dry enough to burn in the fireplace.

What were you thinking that night, Cass? Maybe she'd fallen asleep at the wheel. Of all the possibilities, he preferred this one. That she'd been asleep and never woken up. Never suffered.

Not like Jay, who had bled to death in a mall parking lot. But his suffering was over now. Had been over for a long, long time.

Pierce went to the kitchen to grab Georgia's portable phone. The scent of Christmas—sweet cinnamon and ginger—clung to the air in here. He noticed a basket on the table, filled with cookies and covered in clear plastic film. Tucked underneath was a card. He pulled it out a few inches and saw, printed in Georgia's open, rounded letters, his own name.

Why hadn't she given this to him? He remembered how angry she'd seemed when he'd driven her
to work this last time and guessed she'd finally given
up on him.

Well, good for her.

He closed his eyes for a second, then dialed the
number that Georgia had given him earlier. Georgia's
father answered.

"Yes, Merry Christmas to you, too, sir. Georgia's
fine. She's sleeping right now. We had her checked
out before I drove her home and she's going to be all
right."

"What happened, young man? Her mother and I
don't understand."

Pierce wandered to the back window and surveyed the yard. The trees and shrubs were coated
with white. The snow on the fence caps looked about
five inches thick.

"It's a long story, sir. About a month ago Georgia
started to receive roses from one of her listeners. He
left these roses for her everywhere—on her car, at her
home and at work."

"That sounds a little weird."

"Yes, we called the police. And I installed a security system at her house."

When her father tried to thank him, Pierce cut him
off. After all, he hadn't done enough, had he? Georgia's stalker had still gotten to her.

"At least the creep is in custody now," he concluded, thankful that this was true. If he'd been five minutes later getting to Georgia's studio, the story might have ended much differently.

"Well, you keep an eye on our girl for us."

"I will, sir. I'll keep a very close watch."

Georgia's father sounded relieved. And grateful. Which only made Pierce feel guilty. He didn't deserve this man's trust. He tried to end the call, but then Georgia's mother wanted to talk to him.

Like her husband, she thanked him, over and over. "You must be a special friend," she said. "I hope you'll come and visit us on the farm sometime."

Pierce tried to imagine himself at a dairy farm in South Dakota. He pictured a kitchen table groaning with food, work boots piled up at the back door, a window view of a whitewashed barn and land spreading out on all sides to the horizon.

"That's very kind of you," he said, trying to avoid making a commitment he knew he could never keep.

WHEN GEORGIA OPENED her eyes four hours later, Pierce had a bowl of chicken soup ready for her.

"That smells good."

"It's just from a can," he apologized. Actually, he'd been surprised to find one in her cupboards. Georgia seemed to be the sort of woman who would make her chicken soup from stock she'd boiled herself.

"I can't believe I'm hungry." She accepted the tray and started eating right away.

"So you're feeling okay?"

"Much better. My head doesn't even hurt any-more. And thank God I can think clearly again. Those drugs he gave me—they were just awful. But then I think twice before I take a painkiller, so I'm probably more susceptible than most."

She ate some more. When the bowl was empty, he removed the tray and set it on the night table. He saw her gaze drop to her alarm clock. Her frame seemed to slump a little when she saw the time.

"You would have been home by now," he observed. She nodded.

"I'm sorry your Christmas has been ruined."

Silently she looked at him. He'd never seen her blue eyes so grave.

"I'm sorry he got to you, Georgia. I figured things out just a few hours too late." If he'd been smarter, Monty would never have had the chance to deliver that last rose. He was just lucky he'd gotten into the building before Greenfield had managed to get her to his car. How long would it have taken him to find them if that had happened? And what would Geor-gia have suffered in the interim?

"You're imagining the worst, aren't you?" Geor-gia swung her legs out of the bed.

He hoped she didn't care that he'd pulled off her trousers before tucking her in, but she didn't seem to even think about how she'd ended up in bed with only a shirt and her underwear. With a complete lack of self-consciousness, she now unbuttoned that shirt. He looked away, but not before glimpsing the red bra that matched her panties.

Christmas underwear?

She walked past him to open a dresser drawer from which she pulled a pair of low-riding sweatpants, black with white trim down the side of each leg.

Fascinated, he couldn't stop himself from watching her put them on. Then, a matching hooded top that zippered up the front.

She turned to face him, hands on her hips. "But the worst didn't happen. I'm here and I'm okay. So you didn't fail. Not that it was your job to keep me safe, anyway. Just like it wasn't your job to protect your wife twenty-four-hours a day, or your brother."

She stopped, expectant, but he didn't know what to say. "You're still mad at me, right?"

"Oh, Pierce." She sighed, turned to her mirror, then sighed again. "I should have had a bath—look at this hair."

There was caked blood where she'd hit her head on the filing cabinet, as well as a greenish bruise on the left side of her face.

"Let me take care of that." He led her to the bathroom and had her sit on a stool by the tub. "Take off the jacket, then lean over."

Her eyes were on his as she slowly lowered the zipper, then slipped the jacket off her shoulders. He didn't say a word. Her red bra was smooth satin, low cut with lacy straps.

He took the shower wand and with gentle pressure and warm water, rinsed through her blond curls. He turned off the water, massaged in some shampoo, then rinsed again.

"Cream rinse, please." She handed him the bottle and he went through the whole routine again.

When he was finished, he wrapped her hair in a towel then handed her the jacket.

"Give me a minute to brush my teeth."

He went back to the bedroom for the tray, then carried the dirty dishes to the kitchen. A few minutes later Georgia joined him there. She'd brushed out her wet curls and put some pale gloss on her lips.

"Coffee?" He held up the full pot.

For the first time that morning she smiled.

They sat quietly at the table for a while. "I guess I should be going…."

"Do you?"

He was surprised by the challenge in her tone.

"I suppose you have commitments," she continued. "After all, it is Christmas."

"I have no commitments."

"Then why do you have to go?"

She was driving him crazy. She kept looking at him as if she were waiting for him to say something. But what?

"You know what, Pierce? I'm tired of trying to

figure you out. You risk life and limb to rescue me from Monty Greenfield, you drive me home, put me to bed, sit by that bed for hours waiting for me to wake up, make me chicken soup, look at my body as if you'd like to devour it, then tell me you have to go."

She folded her hands together and rested them on the kitchen table. "Does that seem like a logical sequence of events to you?"

"What do you expect from me? I can't sit here for one more minute without—"

"What? Kissing me? Touching me?"

"Yes, damn it! Yes!"

"So do it."

She was making this too easy. Why did she always make this so easy? "It won't work, Georgia. Not long-term. Not like you deserve."

"It will if you let it. Pierce, why can't you let go of this false picture you have of yourself? You're as capable of loving as the next person."

She would say that. She didn't know. She didn't understand.

"You can't look in the mirror without seeing a man who failed his brother, then his wife. But do you want to know what I see when I look at you?"

She didn't wait for him to answer. "I see a man who stood vigilantly by his wife's bed for four days straight while she was in a coma. I see someone who hired a forty-five-year-old woman with no job skills so that she could provide for her son. I see someone I would give my life for, as I know he would do for me."

"God, Georgia…" He couldn't stand to see the raw emotion in her eyes for another second. She'd left herself so open. Where did she find the courage? And did he have that kind of courage in him?

"You're right about one thing," he said finally. "I would give my life for you. I hope you believe that."

"I do. I absolutely do."

Outside, the snow was still falling. There were six inches on the fence posts now. How many snowflakes did it take to make six inches worth of snow?

"I do love you." It wasn't as hard to say the words as he'd thought it would be. He turned to look at her. "But will it be enough?"

"Enough for what?"

"Enough for you. For a lifetime." He couldn't see anything else but a lifetime for Georgia.

She took his hands. "Look at me, Pierce. I'm happy now. What you're giving me right now, just being in my kitchen, is enough."

Her words were like the snowflakes, accumulating to the point that they covered the world. A hundred words from Georgia. A hundred love songs listened to in the middle of the night. Any man would crumble.

"Georgia." He leaned across the table to kiss her.

CHAPTER NINETEEN

"I CAN'T BELIEVE it's Christmas," Georgia said. "It just doesn't feel like it."

Pierce traced her profile with the tip of his finger. They'd been in bed for hours, but yes, she was right, it was still Christmas.

"It seems so unreal. I haven't had a single eggnog, I won't be eating turkey, or singing carols around the piano—"

"Are you homesick?"

"Truthfully?"

She rolled onto her side to face him. She was so beautiful.

"Yes," he said.

"I've never been happier."

She beamed a smile at him and he had to believe that she meant it.

"Me, too."

"I'm so glad to hear that. Let's change this music. I need something cheery."

"Actually, maybe we should get up now."

"Are you sure? I was thinking maybe dinner in

bed…." She posed for him, a picture in her red bra and panties. When had she put those back on?

But he couldn't let her distract him. It was five-thirty already. "What about Fred? Don't you think we should see how he's doing?"

"You're right. I can't believe I forgot about Fred." She grabbed her sweat suit from the floor. "Give me ten minutes to bathe and change."

"Good idea." He scooped the clothes from her hand. "But maybe you should wear something a little…dressier. It is Christmas, after all."

IT SEEMED ODD that Pierce would comment on her choice of clothing. It was even odder that he had remembered about Fred before she had. As she made good on her promise to bathe quickly, Georgia marveled at how happy she felt. The first time they'd made love had been magical. But today, with Pierce whispering "I love you" in her ear, every kiss and every touch had been that much sweeter.

When she was finished in the bathroom, Georgia took her makeup to the bedroom so Pierce could have a quick cleanup, too. By six o'clock, they were ready.

"I hope we won't be interrupting his dinner," Georgia worried. "I roasted a turkey breast for him a few days ago, and made a little batch of stuffing and some mashed potatoes, so I imagine he'll be eating that."

"I'm sure he'll be glad for some company," Pierce said, urging her out the door with a hand to her back.

"But what about us? What will we eat?"

"Let's think about that after we wish Fred a merry Christmas."

On the porch, Georgia stopped and took in a deep breath of air. "Doesn't that smell like roasting turkey to you?"

"I'm not surprised. Everyone on the block must be cooking the same thing tonight."

"True."

Pierce rapped on Fred's door and it was answered right away. By Sylvie Moreau.

Georgia put a hand to the tender spot on her head. What was going on here? "Sylvie? Is Fred here?"

"Merry Christmas, and yes, Fred is here." Sylvie handed them both a glass of eggnog, with nutmeg grounds on top. "He's stirring gravy in the kitchen."

Georgia stepped into the familiar living room, feeling completely disoriented. Through the arched opening ahead of her, she noticed Brady Walsh setting the table. His mother, Annette, was helping him.

"Hi, Georgia," he said shyly. "Merry Christmas."

"Georgia! Pierce!" Fred came out of the kitchen, a huge grin on his face. He had a tea towel tucked into his belt and wore the tie she'd given him for Christmas. "About time you two made it. Dinner's almost ready."

"What's going on here?" Georgia searched both Pierce's and Fred's faces for answers. Both looked so pleased, it was clear some planning had gone on while she'd been sleeping.

"We're having a party." Fred held up his arms in a welcoming gesture. "It was Pierce's idea. He phoned to tell me about your Christmas plans going awry. He said he knew a few people who would probably be alone for the holiday. Why didn't I try to gather them together?"

"It was a wonderful, gracious idea," Annette Walsh said. "Brady and I were not looking forward to spending the day alone in our big house. I was delighted to contribute our turkey to the feast."

"I'm just about to carve it," Fred said. "It looks delicious."

"What a marvelous idea." Georgia looked fondly at Brady, remembering all his late-night calls. He'd sounded so lonely. But as she'd guessed, it hadn't really been about the girl.

"And Sylvie brought a pumpkin pie for dessert," Fred said, drawing forward the woman who had known Monty Greenfield.

"I couldn't believe it when I saw your face in the producer's control room," Georgia said. "And Monty—he reacted as if he'd seen a ghost."

"He probably felt that way. I've been told I look like my mother."

"He confessed to me what he did to her. I'm so sorry." Georgia gave the woman a hug.

"I'm glad the police have finally caught him. I hope he'll pay for what he did to you, if not for what he did to my mother."

"The police still may be able to make a case for Nancy's murder," Pierce said. "Not so much time has passed. And the doctors and nurses who cared for her will be easy to find."

"Enough of that for now," Fred insisted. "Today is Christmas, after all. Pierce, come help me with the turkey. Georgia, run next door and get us some music, okay?" He winked at Brady. "Maybe you should help her."

LATER THAT NIGHT, listening to Handel's *Messiah* by the Christmas tree in her darkened living room with Pierce, Georgia knew that she would never forget anything about her first Seattle Christmas.

With his arm around her shoulders, Pierce leaned in close to whisper in her ear.

"It's after midnight, Georgia. Do you know what that means?"

She smiled. "No. What does it mean?"

"Time for bed." He stood and pulled her off the couch. "Seattle can't have you tonight, sweetheart. Tonight you're all mine."

"Tonight and always," she promised. Then followed him up the stairs.

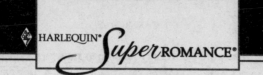

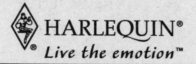

Visit Dundee, Idaho, with bestselling author

brenda novak

A Home of Her Own

Her mother always said if you couldn't be rich, you'd better be Lucky!

When Lucky was ten, her mother, Red—the town hooker—married Morris Caldwell, a wealthy and much older man.

Mike Hill, his grandson, feels that Red and her kids alienated Morris from his family. Even the old man's Victorian mansion, on the property next to Mike's ranch, went to Lucky rather than his grandchildren.

Now Lucky's back, which means Mike has a new neighbor. One he doesn't want to like...

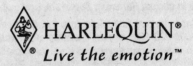

HARLEQUIN®
Live the emotion™

www.eHarlequin.com

HSRH001204

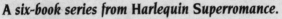

HARLEQUIN *Super*ROMANCE®

A six-book series from Harlequin Superromance.

WOMEN *in Blue*

Six female cops battling crime and corruption on the streets of Houston. Together they can fight the blue wall of silence. But divided, will they fall?

Coming in December 2004,
The Witness by Linda Style
(Harlequin Superromance #1243)

She had vowed never to return to Houston's crime-riddled east end. But Detective Crista Santiago's promotion to the Chicano Squad put her right back in the violence of the barrio. Overcoming demons from her past, and with somebody in the department who wants her gone, she must race the clock to find out who shot Alex Del Rio's daughter.

Coming in January 2005,
Her Little Secret by Anna Adams
(Harlequin Superromance #1248)

Abby Carlton was willing to give up her career for Thomas Riley, but then she realized she'd always come second to his duty to his country. She went home and rejoined the police force, aware that her pursuit of love had left a black mark on her file. Now Thomas is back, needing help only she can give.

Also in the series:
The Partner by Kay David (#1230, October 2004)
The Children's Cop by Sherry Lewis (#1237, November 2004)

And watch for:
She Walks the Line by Roz Denny Fox (#1254, February 2005)
A Mother's Vow by K.N. Casper (#1260, March 2005)

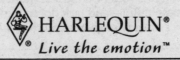

HARLEQUIN®
Live the emotion™

www.eHarlequin.com   HSRWOMIB1204